SACRIFICED TO THE DRAGON

(Stonefire Dragons #1)

Jessie Donovan

Sacrificed to the Dragon
Copyright © 2014 Laura Hoak-Kagey
Mythical Lake Press, LLC
Third Paperback Edition

Cover Art by Clarissa Yeo of Yocla Designs.

ISBN 13: 978-1942211044

To Anne McCaffrey

My teenage years would've been incomplete without her dragonrider stories. I also wouldn't be a writer today without her; she was, and still is, the biggest single influence on my writing career.

Other Books by Jessie Donovan

Stonefire Dragons
Sacrificed to the Dragon
Seducing the Dragon
Revealing the Dragons
Healed by the Dragon
Reawakening the Dragon
Loved by the Dragon (Nov 2015)

Lochguard Highland Dragons
The Dragon's Dilemma
The Dragon Guardian (Feb 2016)

Asylums for Magical Threats
Blaze of Secrets
Frozen Desires
Shadow of Temptation
Flare of Promise (March 2016)

Cascade Shifters
Convincing the Cougar
Reclaiming the Wolf
Cougar's First Christmas
Resisting the Cougar

CHAPTER ONE

Melanie Hall sat in the reception area of the Manchester Dragon Affairs office, tapping her finger against her arm, and wishing they'd hurry the hell up. She'd been sitting for nearly an hour, and with each minute that ticked by, she started to doubt her eligibility. If she didn't qualify to sacrifice herself to one of the British dragon-shifter clans, her younger brother would die; only the blood of a dragon could cure her brother's antibiotic-resistant CRE infection.

A woman dressed in a gray suit emerged from the far doorway and walked toward her. When she reached Mel, the woman said, "Are you Melanie Hall?" Mel nodded, and the woman turned. "Then follow me."

This is it. Mel rubbed her hands against her black trousers before she stood up and followed the woman. They went down one dull, poorly lit corridor and then turned left to go down another. The woman in the gray suit finally stopped in front of a door that read "Human Sacrifice Liaison" and turned the doorknob. Rather than enter, the middle-aged woman motioned for Mel to go inside. She obeyed, and as soon as she entered the room, the door slammed shut behind her.

A man not much older than her twenty-five years sat at a desk piled high with folders and papers. The room couldn't be bigger than ten feet by ten feet, but it felt even smaller since every available space on the walls was decorated with different maps of the UK. Some were partitioned into five sections, while others had little pins pushed into them. She had no idea what the pins stood for, but the map divided into five represented the five dragon-shifter clans of the United Kingdom—two in England, one in Scotland, one in Northern Ireland, and one in Wales.

One of which might soon be her home for the next six months.

The man cleared his throat and she moved her attention from the walls to his face. When she met his blue eyes, he said, "Take a seat."

Mel sat down in the faded plush chair in front of his desk and waited in silence. She had a tendency to say the wrong thing at the wrong time, and while she usually didn't mind, right now it could end up costing her brother his life.

The man picked up a file folder and scanned something inside with his eyes, and then set it down. She wanted to scream for him to tell her the results, but she bit the inside of her cheek to hold her tongue.

The man's almost bored voice finally filled the room. "Ms. Hall, the genetic testing results say that you are compatible with dragon-shifter DNA and should have no problem conceiving one of their offspring. You also cleared all of the extensive psychological tests. If you're still interested in sacrificing yourself, we can begin the final interview."

Mel blinked. Despite her chances being one in a thousand that she could bear a dragon-shifter child, she qualified. Her younger brother would get the needed dragon's blood and be able to live out a long life free of pain; he now had a future.

Tears pricked her eyes and she closed them to prevent herself from breaking down. *Pull yourself together, Hall.* Crying was the last thing she wanted to do right now. She couldn't give the man any reason to dismiss her as a candidate.

"Ms. Hall?"

Mel opened her eyes and gave a weak smile. "I'm sorry, sir. I'm just relieved that my brother will live."

"Yes, yes, the exchange. But we have a lot to cover before we get to the contract specifics, so if you're quite composed, I'll carry on." Mel sat up straight in her chair and nodded. The man continued. "Right. You are healthy, genetically compatible, fertile, unattached, and not a virgin, which are the five requirements needed to qualify. Sacrificing yourself means that you will go to live with Clan Stonefire for a period of six months, and be assigned a temporary male. You will consent to his sexual attentions, and if you become pregnant, you understand that your stay will be extended until after the child is born. If you have any questions, any at all, now is the time to ask them."

She had heard the basics before, but now that she'd passed all of the tests, panic squeezed her heart. As much as she wanted to save her brother—and she would save him—being assigned to have sex with an unknown male dragon-shifter was more than a little scary. Especially since many human women died in the process of birthing half dragon-shifter babies.

If the death-by-baby aspect wasn't bad enough, she was putting her life on hold to do this. Mel was one thesis away from earning her PhD in Social Anthropology. If she became pregnant and survived the delivery, she wasn't sure she could just give up the child and walk away. Most of the women sacrifices who lived past the delivery did abandon their children, but no matter how different the dragon-shifters were from humans, Mel wouldn't be one of them. Family meant everything to her.

And if she didn't give up her child, she would have to give up her dreams in order to spend the rest of her life with Clan Stonefire.

She took a deep breath and remembered her brother Oliver, pale and thin in his sickbed, and her worry dissipated to a manageable level. Even if she became a mother before she'd planned, she would do it three times over to give Oliver a chance to see past his fifteenth birthday.

Still, she wasn't about to pass up this opportunity to ask some questions. The dragon-shifters were extremely private, rarely sharing anything that happened on their land with the public. "I understand consenting to sexual activity, as my main purpose is to help repopulate the dragon-shifters, but what guarantees are in place to ensure I'm not abused or neglected?"

The man leaned back in his chair and steepled his fingers in front of him. "I understand your concern, but the UK Department of Dragon Affairs conducts routine inspections and interviews. Childbearing-related mortality aside, over the last ten years, only one sacrifice has ever reported harsh treatment out of hundreds."

With colossal effort, she managed not to think about her fifty-fifty chance of surviving childbirth. "And what about my friends and family? Can I communicate with them?"

"Communication is forbidden for the first six weeks. After that, it is entirely up to your assigned male as to whether you can communicate or not. From experience, the women who made the greatest effort to conceive were awarded the most privileges."

Right. So if she became a sex goddess, she could talk with her family. How she was going to accomplish that since her previous boyfriends had told her she was "good enough" but never fantastic, she had no idea. But she would cross that bridge when she came to it. "And lastly, when will my brother receive his treatment and when will I leave for the dragons' compound?"

"Once our legal representative has gone through the contract with you and it's been signed and witnessed, a copy will be sent to Clan Stonefire. They should approve it within a matter of days and deliver the vial of dragon's blood to your brother's physician. Normally, you'd be expected to arrive within a week. However, in the case of dying relatives, you're given two weeks to set your affairs in order and to be assured that your brother is recovering. Our office will notify you of the particulars within the next five days."

The man picked up a pen and signed something inside the manila folder on his desk. He picked up a piece of paper and held it out to her. "Since you've had a rational conversation without breaking down or bursting into tears, I think you're mentally sound enough to be sacrificed. If you have no further questions, you can proceed to the legal department."

Even at this late stage of the application process, she now understood how some candidates might be scared off. Hearing about no communication with the outside world as well as how giving birth to a half-dragon baby might kill you was a lot to take in. But Melanie wasn't doing this for herself. Oliver had had a shitty last few years fighting off cancer only to beat it and end up with a drug-resistant infection that was slowly killing him.

Her funny, clever brother deserved a chance to live and enjoy life.

She reached out and took the paper. She said, "Thank you. I'm still interested. Please tell me where the legal department is located, and I'll go there straightaway."

He gave her the directions. Mel thanked the man before leaving his office and making the necessary turns. As she approached the last turn, she glanced down at the paper in her hands. Toward the bottom of the sheet, the man had checked "approved" and signed his name. Seeing it in black and white made her stomach flip.

In less than two weeks, she would go to live with the dragon-shifters and be expected to have sex with one of their males.

She took a deep breath and pushed back the sense of panic. While she didn't know how her assigned dragonman would treat her, there was one thing she had to look forward to—the men were rumored to be fit and muscled. For once in her life, Melanie would get to sleep with a strong, hot man. She only hoped he wouldn't be a complete bastard.

~ ~ ~

Tristan MacLeod knocked on the cottage door of Stonefire's clan leader. When he heard a muffled, "Come in," he twisted the knob and entered.

Bram Moore-Llewellyn, Stonefire's clan leader and Tristan's friend of nearly thirty years, sat behind the old, sturdy oak desk that had been used by leaders of the clan for over a hundred years. It was beat up with more than a few scratches from young dragon-shifters trying out their talons. Tristan thought it looked like shit, but dragons were big on tradition and Stonefire's clan leader was no exception.

Bram motioned for Tristan to come in and sit in one of the wooden chairs in front of his desk. Shutting the door, Tristan complied.

While he had a feeling he knew what this meeting was about, he asked, "You wanted to see me?"

Bram put aside the papers he'd been reading and looked up at him. "It's time, Tristan."

Fuck. "Can't one of the volunteer males have another turn? Putting me together with a human is a bad idea, Bram, and you know it."

Bram leaned back in his chair and shook his head. "No. I can't risk the gene pool getting too small. Neither you nor your sister has had any young, and since you're the elder, you're first in line. I hate to be a hardass, but if you refuse to pair with the latest human sacrifice, I'll have to kick you out of the clan."

"Right, and put me at the mercy of the dragon hunters. I don't really have a choice, do I?"

"No. But since I'm more than just your leader, and I'm also your friend, I waited until a decent candidate came along before I chose you." Bram shuffled through a stack of papers, found what he was looking for, and held it out to Tristan. "Read her mini-summary."

As much as he didn't want to do it, Tristan took the paper and read the one paragraph summary:

Melanie Hall is a twenty-five year old female. Her reason for volunteering as a sacrifice is to heal her brother from a life-threatening disease. Currently, she is a PhD candidate in Social Anthropology at the University of Manchester. Her main interest is the history of human-dragon relations. Her psychological interview showed her to be a strong-willed, determined, and loyal individual who places family above all else. The Dragon Affairs office recommends pairing her with a likewise strong male to avoid unintended manipulation.

He looked up. "So rather than give me a female who will just let me fuck her and walk away, you're giving me one that will probably fight me every step of the way? Are you sure you're my friend?"

Bram smiled. "She'll be good for you. A weaker willed human who would let you fuck her and walk away would prevent you from overcoming your prejudice against humans."

Tristan narrowed his eyes. "Don't bring my dead mother into this."

Bram's smile faded. "It's my job to help you, and by extension, strengthen our clan. You can't keep hiding yourself away by spending all of your time training the young dragons. It's been ten years, Tristan. You need to let it go and focus on what you can do in the here and now, which is to help our clan—and all dragon-shifters, for that matter—from going extinct."

"It's not my bloody fault our numbers are so low. The humans hunted us for thousands of years. The only reason any of the human governments created protections for us over the last two decades is because of the deal we made when we exposed the secret of our blood, to end the AIDS epidemic of the 1980s. To this day, they only value us for the healing properties of our blood and are willing to throw women our way, even if it means possibly killing them in childbirth, to get it."

"I don't care about any of that. Let them value us for our blood. In the meanwhile, the dragon-shifters need to repopulate so that one day we don't need to rely on this barter system to survive." Bram pierced him with his blue-eyed alpha stare. "Now, read the damn contract and sign it. Our healers are waiting for you to shift so they can draw the necessary amount of blood to complete our end of the agreement."

Tristan could refuse and walk away. Despite the shitty odds, he would probably do just that if it were only him. But he couldn't abandon his sister Arabella; especially as he was the only family she had left.

And damn Bram, he knew that.

Tristan held out his hand. "Give me the bloody contract. But if you think this is going to magically cure my hatred of humans, you're in for a surprise."

His friend handed over the papers. "We'll see, Tristan. We'll see."

CHAPTER TWO

Melanie stood with her parents in front of the well-guarded entrance to Stonefire's land. She knew someone from the clan would arrive at any minute to take her inside, but saying goodbye to her parents was harder than she'd imagined. She was a grown woman, for crying out loud. Yet as she looked from her mom to her dad and back again, she realized this might be the last time she ever saw them, unless her assigned male granted her privileges. Yeah, the idea of a male being in charge of what she could and couldn't do didn't sit well with her, but she'd have to suck it up if she wanted to survive.

She really couldn't say anything to ease their worry, and she'd never been good at lying. Still, she forced a smile and decided to stretch the truth a little. "Mom, Dad, it'll be all right. Just look after Oliver for me. I expect a full report once I have access to a phone line again."

Her dad cupped her cheek. "I know everything is done, but I wish you would've talked to us about this, Mel. We could've found another way."

She stared at her father with his slightly balding head and wire rim glasses, careful to burn the image into her memory. "You know there was no other way. Without an injection of dragon's blood, Oliver would have died. I'm aware of the risks in doing this, and Dad, I'm more than old enough to make my own decisions."

"I know, love. But we're going to miss you on the annual summer holiday to Scotland this year."

She might be a grown woman, but her family had a tradition that Mel still looked forward to. Every year they took a trip to Scotland, and every year they visited a different castle. Her parents were determined to visit each and every one before they died, and the thought of her missing out on the trip for the first time in over twenty-years made her chest tighten.

Mel cleared her throat. "Just make sure it's one of the dodgy, crap castles, and then I won't be that upset to miss it."

Her British dad then pulled her into a hug, the action very much the influence of Mel's American mother. He murmured against her hair, "I love you, Mel-bell, and I don't know how I'll ever thank you for saving Oliver's life."

Mel squeezed and stepped back from her father. "Just take care of him." She looked over to her mother, who was being unusually quiet. "Mom?"

Without saying a word, her mother rushed over and embraced her. Mel closed her eyes and held her mom tight, memorizing the light lilac scent of her mother's lotion before saying, "I love you, Mom."

"I love you too, dear." Her mother pulled back and took Mel's face in her hands. "You can call us and let us know about anything, anything at all, once you have access to a phone."

She fought the tears in her eyes and forced a smile. "Of course."

Her mother's face went stern. "I mean it. I don't care if my grandchild ends up being half-dragon, I will love him or her with all of my heart."

At that remark, tears started to roll down Mel's cheeks. "You don't know how much that means to me, Mom."

Her mother patted her cheek. "I don't care what the rest of the world thinks; my family comes first, no matter what their genetic heritage."

Mel pulled her mother into another hug. While pregnancy was highly likely, she'd been afraid her parents wouldn't approve if she did have a child. But she should have known better than to doubt her parents.

She had taken them for granted all these years. If she survived the birth and ever got out, she'd treasure them, as they deserved to be treasured.

A deep, unfamiliar male voice spoke up behind her. "Ms. Melanie Hall?"

Mel pulled away from her mom and wiped her eyes with the sleeve of her cardigan before she turned around to find a tall man with dark hair and eyes, looking at her and her parents with what could only be called suspicion. The thick, black tattoo that crawled out from beneath his short sleeves to just above his elbow told her the man was a dragon-shifter.

The only question was whether he was to be her dragon-shifter or not.

Regardless, she had decided over the last two weeks that she wouldn't be afraid of them unless they gave her a reason. Even then, she'd do everything in her power not to show her fear. She had a feeling the dragon-shifters would appreciate a show of strength.

She squared her shoulders and raised her chin. "That's me."

"I'll give you three minutes to say your final goodbyes. Come to me when you're done."

SACRIFICED TO THE DRAGON

With that, the man went over to a patch of trees, crossed his arms over his chest, and stared. Even from fifteen feet away, she felt the intensity of his gaze, and she was starting to understand how most women would freak out at it. However, Mel had dealt with worse during her part-time jobs all throughout university; first at a bar and later at a restaurant. A grumpy, verbally stunted jerk would be like a walk in the park in comparison.

Determined not to waste what precious time she had left with her family, Mel turned back to her parents and tried to ignore the heat of the dragon-shifter's gaze that was undoubtedly still trained on her back.

~~~

Tristan watched the short, curvy woman with reddish brown hair and green eyes as she hugged her parents. She was a bit rounder and softer than the females of his people, but at first glance, he didn't find it unappealing. The woman's tits alone should be able to get his cock hard enough to do his job.

Provided he could get her naked first. He wouldn't force her, but thanks to Bram's choice of sacrifice, it was probably going to take more than a few caresses to get her willing. He glared in Melanie's direction as down payment for the trouble the woman was going to cause him.

If Bram thought Tristan was going to turn into a gentle, flattering male for the human female, his clan leader was in for a surprise. The human female was here for one purpose, and one purpose only—to breed. He'd do his duty and fuck her until she became pregnant. Then he could go back to his life until the child was born. If she managed to survive the birth, he could only hope the woman would flee back to the humans and leave the child's upbringing to him.

Like most dragon-shifters, Tristan cherished the gift of children, even if his would be half-human.

However, he was getting ahead of himself. Melanie would have a two-day adjustment period before she was required to have sex with him. He just wanted to hurry up and get it over with. But he'd signed the sacrifice contract and he wouldn't embarrass his clan by breaking it.

The woman's time was up. He was about to go fetch her when she gave a wave to her parents, picked up her suitcase, and strutted toward him. He'd discovered one thing about her—she was punctual.

When she was only a few feet away, he put out a hand. "I can carry your bag."

She shook her head. "I don't even know your name, so how am I supposed to trust you with my things?"

No matter how much trouble it'd be later, he still preferred feisty to whimpering or scared shitless. "I'm Tristan MacLeod of Clan Stonefire."

She peered up at him with her light green eyes and Tristan frowned. Why were human women so short?

Melanie stared at him for another two seconds before she offered him her bag. "That still doesn't really tell me who you are, but since I'm staying with Stonefire for at least the next six months, I can hunt you down if you run off with my things."

He pierced her with a stare. "If I decided to run off with your suitcase, I guarantee you wouldn't be able to find me. I have wings."

"Right. You're a dragon. I'm not sure how I forgot about that." She offered her bag again. "Well, take it then. I'd say it's heavy, but you look like you can handle it."

She'd forgotten he was a dragon? *Fuck.* So much for using the rumors of dragon brutality to get her to leave him alone. The female was going to be a bigger challenge than he'd anticipated. His preemptive glare had been justified.

For now, he just needed to deliver her to his clan leader. He could worry about how much trouble she was later.

He took her bag. "We have a meeting. Follow me."

He turned and started walking. Since he didn't try to pace his strides with her much shorter ones, she had to half-jog to keep up. *Good.* Maybe if he kept her winded, she wouldn't try talking to him. He had no intention of getting to know Ms. Melanie Hall.

~ ~ ~

Melanie wasn't sure what she had expected on meeting her first dragon-shifter face-to-face, but Tristan MacLeod hadn't been it.

Yes, he was tall, lean, and muscular—okay, she'd admit sexy—but he could probably snap her in two if he tried. Manners and politeness definitely weren't his forte. She doubted he even knew how to smile.

And yet, she had a sinking feeling he was the male who had been assigned to her.

Best not to jump to conclusions, Hall. Right. She was a social scientist. She needed to observe and obtain more information before forming any sort of definitive opinion. Maybe the dragonman was merely having a bad day.

At least, the walk was doing some good to help calm the fluttering in her stomach. She might've put on a brave front for the dragon-shifter, but inside her heart thumped a million beats a minute.

And she'd only been on the dragon-shifter's land for ten minutes. How could she last six months?

Taking a deep breath, Mel remembered her decision to treat her time with the dragon-shifters as nothing more than a difficult fieldwork assignment.

Observing Clan Stonefire as an anthropologist was going to be her coping technique. Yes, she would have to get naked with some dragonman and possibly bear his half-dragon child, but she was going to make the most of her six months here, or longer. If she played her cards right, she might be able to write her doctoral thesis on something to do with the Stonefire dragons.

She'd been struggling to come up with a good thesis idea, but a close study on how the dragon-shifters lived would be groundbreaking since very few true facts were known about them. In Mel's opinion, giving humans a glimpse into their daily lives might help ease the fear surrounding the dragon clans. Far too many parents still told legends of how dragons would swoop down and pluck children from their parents to eat them as part of the nighttime story routines.

A sound that was a mixture of an eagle's cry and a lion's roar echoed through the air. Mel stopped in her tracks as she clapped her hands over her ears against the noise. Before she could look up to see what had caused it, she had to close her eyes against the wind as it whooshed over her. Two seconds later, she opened her eyes to see the receding shapes of a gold and red dragon fade into the distance. She could only make out their wings and large bodies before they disappeared from her line of sight, and disappointment rushed over her. One of the perks of living with the dragon-shifters was that she could finally see a dragon up close, but it looked like it wasn't going to happen quite yet.

She looked over and saw Tristan standing with her bag. Before she could stop herself, she asked, "Do you ever take humans up with you when you're in dragon form?"

His neutral expression became dark. "We're not pack animals at the mercy of human masters."

"That's not what I meant, and you know it."

"You obviously haven't had to deal with dragon hunters or pro-containment activists. Some say that being pack animals or blood donors is all we're good for." He turned and started walking. "Come on. Stonefire's clan leader is waiting for you."

Asshole. Even if he was having a bad day, he didn't have to be so rude.

Mel half-jogged to catch up with him. He was still a foot or two ahead of her, but if he thought it would deter her from continuing their conversation, he was sadly mistaken. Anger had always made her brave—and a little bit careless. "You're right; I don't know much about the poachers or the anti-dragon people. But unless you tell me, I never will."

Tristan stopped and she nearly ran into his back. He looked over his shoulder. "Look, I'm going to lay out the facts for you. While you might've volunteered for this, I didn't and I don't plan to waste my time on getting to know you or some such bullshit. I will do what I'm contracted to do, nothing more. I suggest you gear yourself up for some sex and enjoy it, because that's all you're going to get from me."

Mel blinked. "You're the male assigned to me?"

Tristan turned and gave a mocking bow. "The cream of the crop, my lady."

"Somehow, I doubt it."

There was a flash of hatred in his eyes. "I don't want this any more than you do, but you signed the contract, which means you're going to try to give me a child. And if all goes well, I hope you'll leave me and my child alone and go back to your human life."

He started walking again, and all Mel could do was stare. How in the hell was she supposed to sleep with *him*? She'd tried not to build up any fantasies about her life with the dragon-shifters, but never in a million years had she expected such a bastard to be assigned to her.

Unfortunately, she didn't have a choice; her hands were tied with the contract she'd signed.

Mel clenched her fists at her side and picked up her pace to catch up with Tristan. At least by the terms of her contract, she had two sex-free days to get to know the clan and have her basic questions answered. Somehow, in those two days, she needed to either find out why Tristan hated her so much or try to find a way to transfer the contract to a different dragonman.

Chapter Three

Thankfully, for the rest of the walk to Bram's house, Melanie remained silent.

Tristan had laid out the facts and been as blunt as he could be, but if the stubborn glint in her eye was anything to go on, his brusque manner wasn't going to be enough.

He still couldn't believe her first question about his clan was whether dragons ever took humans up for a ride in the air or not. Even putting aside the fact she didn't know much, if anything, about dragon-shifter ways, would she ask a human male she just met if she could have a piggyback ride?

No. She wouldn't.

Humans felt entitled and had always viewed themselves superior to the "dragon beasts". The restrictive laws in Britain about where they could go or who could visit their land only reinforced that fact.

As a boy, he'd dismissed the tales of human cruelty as nothing more than stories. But then they had tortured and killed his mother and he'd finally understood what monsters they could be.

At least Melanie had reminded him of that fact. A small, very small, part of him had wondered if his assigned female would be different. It was good to know she wasn't.

Since his behavior didn't seem to scare her off, he'd just have to think of other ways to persuade the female to leave either when her time was up or after she gave him a child.

To be honest, he wanted a child. A little male or female to help start a new family. His sister Arabella had been with his mother when the humans had captured her, and to this day, she hadn't forgiven herself for leaving as their mother had begged her to do. But maybe a niece or nephew would finally help her to heal and move on.

Of course, that brought his problem full circle, to the female trailing behind him. Children required sex, and since he wasn't a rapist, he'd have to get creative to get her naked.

The sound of Melanie's half-jogging steps stopped. Wondering what she was doing now, he turned around to see her gaping at the collection of houses and workshops in the clan's central living area. All of the houses were two stories and simple stone or brick, but even if her accent wasn't quite English, she would've seen similar buildings in the little villages she'd passed on her way here.

On closer inspection, he realized that she wasn't staring at the buildings but rather at the commotion going on behind them. The young dragons were practicing their take-offs and landings in the designated safe area.

The sight was an everyday occurrence to him, but not to the human.

But he didn't care. All that mattered was getting her to Bram as fast as possible. He itched to go for a quick flight before the welcoming ceremony and every minute the female wasted watching the young dragons was a minute less of freedom spent in the skies.

Tristan walked over to Melanie and barked, "Stop gawking. We have a meeting with the clan leader."

Her mouth had been hanging open, but she promptly shut it and scowled up at him. "There is nothing in my contract about having to follow your every order." She crossed her arms across her chest and he forced himself not to look at her plumped up breasts. "Just ask me nicely to pick up my pace and see what happens."

Yes, that determined glint was still in her eyes. As much as he wanted to get to Bram's house, he couldn't help but ask, "Why aren't you afraid of me? For most humans, a dragon-shifter barking at them would send them into a fit."

"I'm guessing by your comment that you didn't read my file, so here it is: I'm earning my PhD in Social Anthropology. You do know what anthropology is, don't you?"

He glared, careful not to let his confusion at her change of topic show. "I might be a big beast, but I have a brain. Anthropology is the study of culture."

"Close enough."

"And that has to do with your behavior how, exactly?"

She gestured to their surroundings. "All of this is new to me, and all I want to do is look at every detail and store it away into my memory. New cultures don't scare me, they fascinate me."

Bloody fantastic. His assigned female was going to take a lot of persuading to make her leave at the end of her time. "You can look your fill tomorrow. Right now, you either need to start walking, or I'll use other ways to get you to the meeting."

She pointed a finger at him. "You act all scary and badass, but unless you want to risk your clan's participation in the sacrifice system, you won't hurt me."

She was right; he would never deny the future of his clan that way. Nevertheless, he could do many things without hurting her.

He tossed her bag on the ground. Then he bent over a little, pushed his shoulder against her body, and lifted her.

She squeaked and then demanded, "What are you doing?"

He tightened his grip on her legs and tried to ignore the soft, feminine curves pressed against his body or the way her feminine scent made his inner dragon rumble in appreciation. His dragon said inside his head, *Her softness will be nice. When can we fuck her?*

Shit. He didn't need pressure from his inner beast. *Not now.*

Forcing his dragon-half to the back of his mind, he said, "I'm not going to argue with you or try to be all nice and polite. That's not who I am, and I'm sure as hell not going to change for you. So in the interest of time, I'll just carry you. Your contract allows that."

He started walking. He expected her to struggle, but leave it to the woman to start talking instead. "I have always believed the dragon-shifters weren't the caveman alphas you're all rumored to be, but your behavior has changed that. What are you going to do next? Chain me to a bed?"

"Thanks for giving me the idea, human. Keeping you tied to my bed might speed up the conception process, and then you can go live with the other unmated humans and give us both some peace."

Melanie huffed, but fell quiet. He wasn't sure if he should be relieved or be worried that she was coming up with a way to get back at him. If she kept standing up to him and challenging him at every turn, he might just have to tie her to the bed to keep her out of trouble.

SACRIFICED TO THE DRAGON

~~~

Taking deep breaths in through her nose, Mel tried to calm down. She was aware that she'd fallen into the trap of saying the wrong thing at the wrong time, but the dragonman had a way of stirring her anger. If his words weren't enough, he'd then picked her up and carried her on his shoulder as if it wasn't the twenty-first century, but some far-gone time when women were nothing more than property.

True, she had no idea if women were viewed as property inside the dragon culture. Her research in the last few weeks had turned up very little about the dragon-shifters' gender roles, or much of anything for that matter. But if the females were anything like the male under her stomach, she doubted they'd put up with Tristan's manhandling or any of the rest of his crap.

Mel was clever enough to know fighting him was a waste of time; he could overpower her with one hand. Besides, being this close to his body, she couldn't ignore the amount of heat radiating from the hard muscles of his chest and back, or the way he smelled of the wind and something uniquely masculine.

Before she could do something stupid, such as take a deep inhalation of Tristan's oddly intoxicating scent, he stopped and slowly slid her body down his. Her curves loved the contrasting hardness of his chest, and the friction of their bodies turned her nipples into hard points.

No doubt, the dragonman would use her body's betrayal against her.

The only saving grace was she felt his hard cock poking against her stomach. Despite his earlier comments about humans,

Tristan MacLeod could be aroused by one. Maybe she could use that to her advantage later.

The moment her feet touched the ground, the dragonman released his hold on her body and moved away as if he'd been burned. The mixture of irritation and disgust in his eyes poked at her self-esteem.

Melanie kept her head held high. She knew she wasn't one of the stick thin models who had to watch every damn thing they ate, but she wasn't unhealthy. She cooked everything from scratch and enjoyed her near-daily walks. If he didn't like what he saw, too bad. She wasn't about to let this bastard chip away at her hard-earned self-esteem.

Not caring if her mouth got her in trouble, she said, "Stop treating and eyeing me like a piece of meat."

"Why? You're the one who offered your body to a stranger."

"To save my brother. That makes a world of difference."

He looked unconvinced. "Rationalize all you like, I don't care. All that matters is that your body reacts to mine, which means I won't have to try too hard to get you naked."

"Why, because you're fit? Just because you're tall, dark, and muscled doesn't mean anything. You're mean, cruel, and rude. And that's not attractive."

"Your nipples say differently." He turned and walked the last few paces to the door. "Now, that's enough. It's time to meet my clan leader."

He knocked, opened the door, and entered the stone cottage, leaving her to stand by herself. A few of the dragon-shifters had been watching her exchange with Tristan, and they continued to stare at her. Her cheeks flushed as she realized what they must've overheard.

Great way to make a first impression, Hall. But she couldn't help it. Tristan was like a lighter for her temper.

She took a deep breath and exhaled before she headed for the open cottage door. If she tried hard enough, she might do a better job of making a good impression with Stonefire's leader. Considering she would need his approval to do any sort of write-up about his clan, she needed to temporarily put aside her issues with Tristan and morph back into the pleasant, friendly young woman she was with most people.

Inside the cottage was a large room with a desk in the far corner. Sitting at the desk was another huge, muscled man with a tattoo snaking out from under his t-shirt, signaling he was a dragon-shifter. Soon she might get the chance to see what the dragon-shifter tattoos looked like—with Tristan, at least—without a shirt getting in the way.

Speaking of the bastard, Tristan was already at the desk and speaking in a language she didn't understand. It didn't sound like French, German, or Spanish. Maybe the dragons had their own language, but much like what had happened to Gaelic in Scotland, it had mostly died out over the years and been replaced with English.

To avoid being completely disrespectful to Stonefire's leader, Mel kept quiet as she approached the desk. When she finally stood next to Tristan, the leader stopped talking and fixed her with a stare.

His eyes were a deep blue that pierced right to her soul. She didn't think she could lie to the dragonman, given the chance. While she'd had no problem speaking her mind with Tristan, everything about the man behind the desk suggested she'd better keep quiet if she knew what was good for her.

Without moving his blue gaze from hers, the leader stood up and said, "My name is Bram Moore-Llewellyn."

The man's bearing was so regal she barely resisted the urge to curtsy. "Melanie Hall. Just Hall, I don't have a double-barreled last name like you."

The fierce man didn't even crack a smile. Were all dragon-shifters so serious?

Bram said, "Let's sit down." He then motioned to a set of couches on the far side of the room.

Bram took the couch across while Tristan sat down next to her, careful not to touch her. Mel folded her hands in her lap, unsure if she should speak or wait for one of the men to speak.

When all they did was stare at her, she decided enough was enough. Since any time she talked with Tristan she said whatever came to mind, she focused on Bram. "Sir, Bram, Mr. Moore-Llewellyn? I'm honored to meet you, but if there is nothing else to discuss, may I go? I'd really like the chance to settle in and get to know my surroundings."

Tristan drawled, "More like go back and spy on the young dragons practicing."

She looked over at him. "I think that falls under the 'getting to know my surroundings' criteria."

There was a grunt from Bram's direction, and she looked back at him and he said, "Melanie, you can get to know your surroundings tomorrow since tonight will be busy." He waved toward Tristan. "Tristan will take you to your quarters. Some of the human women will visit with you and prepare you for tonight."

"Tonight?"

Bram nodded. "Yes, tonight. I'm not surprised Tristan didn't tell you about the welcoming ceremony because he hates

34

group gatherings, but you two will have one all the same. It's a chance for the clan to get to know you, and for us to wish you two a fruitful pairing."

Mel's cheeks flushed at the thought of "pairing" with Tristan.

Bram continued. "While I wanted to meet you, there is another reason I asked Tristan to bring you to me. If for any reason you are scared for your safety or are being mistreated, come to me. I trust only a few people more than Tristan, but it's important for you to know you're not alone. You are part of Stonefire—at least, for now—and I do everything I can to protect my clan. Remember that."

At the fierceness in his eyes, she believed him. She nodded, but as the silence dragged on, she said, "Is there anything else?"

Bram eyed her for a minute before he said, "One last thing. If you betray my clan, you will be punished. Some human females in the past have tried to steal dragon's blood or other secrets, and are now serving life sentences in prison. I know this is all forbidden in the fine print of your contract, but I've found a straightforward reminder helps to lessen the number of offenses."

She wondered if just taking notes would fall under the category of stealing secrets. She'd have to talk with Bram about that soon, just in case. "I understand."

Bram stood up. "Good. Now, Tristan will take you to your assigned cottage where you'll live for your time here at Stonefire. I'll see you again tonight." He put out a hand and she took it to shake.

She felt a hand at her elbow. She looked to her left and saw Tristan standing next to her. She hadn't even heard him stand up.

He tugged at her elbow. "Let's go. The females are probably already waiting for you."

Bram released her hand. With a nod, Tristan turned her around and guided her out the door.

As he urged her toward the biggest collection of houses she'd seen so far, some of Mel's bravado faded. Meeting with some of the human women would give her a glimpse of how her life would be here. Given the two males she'd met so far, she didn't have high hopes everything would magically get better once she settled in.

CHAPTER FOUR

Tristan couldn't get Melanie to move fast enough. He wanted to drop her off and get a small reprieve from her incessant questions, and her oddly addicting scent.

Carrying her on his shoulder had been a mistake. The instant her full, plump breasts had pressed against his back, his cock had gone hard. Sliding her down his body had only made him harder.

If that wasn't enough, her scent told him she was nearly at the fertile time of the month, and his inner dragon had screamed at him to throw her on the ground and fuck her. Even now, with Melanie at his side, his dragon was impatient, not understanding why he would give another male the chance to get her with child ahead of him.

Tristan might've grown up the late twentieth and early twenty-first century, but his dragon functioned primarily on instinct. Hunt, fly, fuck, eat. That's what his beast understood.

While every dragon-shifter learned from an early age how to control their dragons, spending two days with a female who was both fertile and who had caught the eye of his dragon would be the ultimate test of self-control. That was why he'd tried to convince Bram in Mersae, the dragon-shifter language, to let someone else show her around Stonefire's land tomorrow. However, Bram had been firm and told him to get his dragon under control. If Tristan couldn't manage to do that, then he wasn't worthy of a female to birth his children.

An hour ago, he would've been happy to give the human sacrifice to someone else. But after feeling Melanie's soft body pressed up against his, the thought of another male taking her made his dragon roar inside his head. When Bram had taken her hand, he'd barely resisted throwing his friend across the room.

The whole situation was fucked up. Bram was his oldest friend and clan leader, but his dragon didn't seem to care. It wanted Melanie. Period. Unless he wanted to unleash an angry, snarling dragon on his clan—losing control of his dragon would get him kicked out or worse—passing her off to another male wasn't an option.

His dragon pushed his way to the front of his mind. *The female is ours. Take her. Bond her. Now.*

He wrestled the beast back and was barely in control again when Melanie's voice interrupted his thoughts. "Are you going to tell me about tonight's event?"

He glanced over at her. The sound of her voice calmed his dragon. For once, he was grateful for the distraction of her questions. "What's there to tell? People will get together, eat, drink, and dance."

"Is that why you don't like big get-togethers? Because you have to dance?"

"No."

She tugged on her elbow but Tristan didn't release his grip. "Well?"

They were almost to her new dwelling, and he decided talking would keep the human part of him front and center. "I don't like contained, crowded places. I'm part dragon, and I much prefer the freedom of the skies."

"But what about airplanes? Or air pollution? I'd imagine flying isn't as grand as it might've once been."

Keep her talking. I want to hear her voice, his dragon told him. Since they were nearly to the cottage, he decided to listen to his beast. "Even with those things, there's nothing like using the power of your wings to soar over an ocean, or a mountain, or a forest. Humans must rely on airplanes, cars, and boats to get them from one place to the other, but as a dragon, I can fly anywhere. My wings are my independence."

He didn't spoil his little speech by saying he could fly almost anywhere. Certain cities had dragonflight bans, and in some rural areas, dragon hunters waited for their prey; harvesting and selling dragon's blood on the black market was becoming a big problem.

Thankfully, they arrived at the small stone cottage sitting a little away from the rest, which meant he wouldn't have to keep talking to her. He nodded his head toward the thatched cottage and said, "This is to be your home while you're here." He could hear the females inside. "The human females will answer your questions and bring you to the ceremony."

She frowned. "And what about you?"

Using the trick of talking to forget about his dragon's instinct seemed to have backfired. He'd been too nice, and Melanie seemed to have gotten her hopes up about him caring about her. It was time to fix that. "I'm going for a quick flight to rid the stench of human from my nose."

His dragon roared and said, *She doesn't stink. Stay. Take her. We will scent her.*

Shut it.

Tristan ignored the hurt in the human's eyes. He couldn't let her like him, or his dragon's need might overwhelm his own self-control. "Until tonight."

He turned and left her standing in the dirt. His dragon growled in irritation at the change of Melanie's scent from one of a soft, warm woman to a hurt, lonely one.

Well, fuck you, dragon. Just because his beast had forgotten that humans had torn apart his family didn't mean Tristan-the-man had.

He picked up his pace and headed toward the clearing where he could shift and take off. He hoped the flight would clear his head and allow him to get a handle on his dragon again, or the next two days were going to be pure hell. No female had ever affected his beast to the point his dragon demanded things of him, and that scared him a little.

~~~

Melanie watched Tristan walk away and tried not to cry. She'd thought they'd made some progress when he'd told her about not liking confined spaces, or about the freedom of flight. But then he'd gone and said she stank.

Even if her body was attracted to him—and it was—she wasn't sure her heart could take having sex with him, especially if all he'd do afterward was tear her down again.

Not now, Hall. She closed her eyes and took a deep breath. She'd only been on Stonefire's land for a little over an hour and it was too soon to start guessing her future.

Opening her eyes, she eyed the cottage door and decided the best thing was to see what the other human women said about their time here. Their experience would be more valuable to her than crying or wondering what if.

Unsure of what she should do, Melanie knocked. A faint "Come in" answered and she opened the door and entered the cottage.

Inside were two women. The one with curly red hair and blue eyes was about Mel's age and very much pregnant. The other one was a little older with long, black hair and dark, golden skin. The woman with the dark hair smiled and said, "I'm Samira." She gestured at the redhead. "And this is Caitriona. Welcome to Stonefire."

Mel forced a smile. "I'm Melanie Hall."

She took a step toward the women when a little boy who looked to be about three years old peeked out from behind Samira's skirts. Samira looked down at the boy with love and placed a hand on his head. "And this is my son, Rhys."

As Samira coaxed her son out and picked him up, Mel looked over at Caitriona. But the woman wasn't smiling. If anything, her vacant expression made her look like a walking zombie. Mel decided Samira would be her best bet for information and looked at the woman holding her son in her arms. "While it's nice to meet you all, I'm hoping you can help me understand what it is I'm supposed to do tonight. What's a welcoming ceremony?"

Samira jostled her son on her hip. "We have enough time to chat over some tea." She looked at Caitriona. "Cait, can you make us some tea and bring out some biscuits?"

Cait nodded and headed for the small kitchen on the far side of the room. Samira motioned her head toward the couches and chairs. "Let's sit down."

41

Mel looked over at Cait. "Shouldn't she sit down? She looks quite pregnant."

Samira walked over and whispered, "She's only six months along. Besides, she likes to keep busy. It helps her to forget her troubles."

Mel wanted to ask more, but when Samira pushed against her shoulder with her own, she took the hint. Once they sat down, Mel on the chair and Samira on the couch opposite with her son on her lap, Samira said, "I'll tell you about the welcoming ceremony in a minute. First, what did you think of Tristan?"

Unsure of Samira's loyalties, she decided to keep her answer diplomatic. "I just met him."

Samira clicked her tongue. "Come, now. He's a broody bastard when it comes to humans. You can say so, and it won't go outside this room. Trust me, being a human amongst the dragon-shifters can be a trial sometimes."

Mel studied the smiling woman holding her son tight in her arms and decided to trust her a little. "That's an understatement." She paused, but before she could stop herself, she said, "I think Tristan hates me."

"It doesn't surprise me."

Mel clenched a fist against her jeans. The other woman knew nothing about her. But Samira continued before she could say a word. "It has nothing to do with you, my dear. You seem lovely. But Tristan's mother was killed by humans, and he's never gotten over it."

She blinked. She'd heard tales of dragon hunters, but like most humans, she'd thought the British government had gotten the illegal poachers under control.

Knowing what had happened to Tristan's mother put an entirely new perspective on things. "But why are you telling me this? I assume his mother's death is a very personal thing, and something he doesn't want strangers to know."

Samira shrugged. "Everyone in the clan knows about it. There's no reason to hide it, especially as Tristan would never mention it to a human, even if you tortured him for a decade."

Wow. To say Tristan had issues was putting it mildly.

Cait came in with a tray and she placed it on the small table between the couch and chairs. The timid woman poured a cup of tea, picked up a cookie, and sat in the chair farthest off to the side. As she nibbled on the cookie, Mel couldn't help but notice her vacant expression and defeated posture. Quite simply, it looked like Cait had given up any chance at happiness.

Before Mel could think better of it, she said, "Cait, what's the matter?"

At first, Mel thought the woman would ignore her. But finally, the redhead spoke, her voice not more than a whisper, "I want to go home."

Cait let out a sob, and Mel went to the woman's side and put her arms around her. When Cait's sobs didn't let up, she glanced over to Samira, who was bouncing her son on her lap to distract the boy from Cait's breakdown.

She focused back on Cait, stroking her hair and making soft noises. Eventually, the woman stopped crying. As Cait wiped her eyes with her hands, Mel forced herself to ask, "Tell me, Cait. Why do you want to go home? Is it really so bad here?"

Cait's eyes went to where Samira was entertaining her son. She looked back to Mel's face and said, "What Samira has is rare. Her dragonman loves her, loves their son, and he would die to protect them. Mine left six months ago, as soon as I was pregnant, and no one's heard of him since." She placed a hand on her belly. "He didn't want a child, but all of the men take at least one turn. I was terrified of him in the beginning, which didn't help matters. But he didn't want me, and he doesn't want our child. I'm tired of the looks of pity and people tiptoeing around me. Everyone here talks, as you'll soon find out, and I just want to go back to being normal."

"What about your baby?"

Cait held her stomach with both hands. "This baby was a way to pay off the debt my ex-husband left me with, nothing more. As soon as it's born, I'm leaving."

Samira's voice interrupted them. "That's enough for now. If we don't get Melanie ready for the welcoming ceremony, we'll hear from Bram. Clean yourself up, Cait. Melanie, come with me."

Samira stood up and went into one of the side rooms. Mel gave Cait one last hug before she followed. Once she was in the room, Samira leaned down to her ear and whispered, "Cait's dragonman was banished for cheating on his sacrifice, yes; but don't let her words poison you. That dragonman had always been a problem. Bram thought he could make him behave, but he was wrong. Don't worry, Tristan is different."

"How, exactly? He wants nothing to do with me."

Samira leaned back enough to meet her eye. "Ask him to take you to his job tomorrow. Then you'll see."

Mel opened her mouth, but Samira turned around and set her son down on the large bed in the room. She went to the side closet, pulled something out, and turned around with an armful of a shimmery light green material. "Right, let's get started."

CHAPTER FIVE

Tristan smoothed the material held around his waist with a belt, tossed the remaining length of fabric over his shoulder, and secured it with a pin. His clothing was similar to the old belted plaids of Scotland except that it was made of a solid dark red wool. Most humans didn't realize that the kilt style had originated with the dragon-shifters first; the garment easily allowed a dragonman to slide the material off his shoulder and shift at a moment's notice.

He left his dwelling and headed for the main hall. His flight had eased some of his tension and calmed his dragon, but as soon as he was within range of Melanie's scent, the battle would start all over again.

Spending all day with her tomorrow was going to be hell. At this rate, he'd be trying to take her at midnight tomorrow.

As he neared the dragon-shifters' former castle with its towering stone keep, crumbling walls, and massive four-story brick building that served as the dragon-shifters' main hall, he could hear conversations in a mixture of English and Mersae, the dragon-language. Nearly everyone, including the children, would attend tonight's gathering. Bram liked to say it was to give everyone a chance to meet the new sacrifice, but Tristan believed it was to show off the new possible threat.

He passed a few of his fellow trainers and nodded a greeting. No one offered any sort of congratulatory remarks, which was to be expected considering the near meltdown of the last female sacrifice eight months ago. Unfortunately, Caitriona Belmont had conceived. And she was still with them. As much as Tristan hated humans, he almost felt pity for her. Neil, her assigned male, had broken the sacrifice contract and disgraced the clan.

Tristan had far too much respect for Bram to do the same.

He pressed through the throngs of people and headed inside to the main raised dais in the front of the room. Bram was already there, but there was no sign of Melanie or Samira, the human female in charge of getting her ready. They were late.

When he was close enough, Bram caught his eye and signaled for him to come up onto the dais. Tristan approached his leader and said, "Did you send someone to check on the human females?"

Bram glanced at him. "Anxious to have your First Kiss?"

"No. I just want to get this over with as quickly as possible."

"You do know that you'll be seeing her again tomorrow. And probably the day after that. While it's my job to scare her a bit into behaving, you need to stop pushing her away if you ever hope to get your cock anywhere near her."

He looked at his friend. "How do you know I'm pushing her away?" Bram raised an eyebrow. "Hey, I'm following my contract to the letter. I won't physically harm her or force her. That's all I care about."

"Harm comes in more than just physical injuries, Tristan. Look at what Neil did to Cait. Words and actions can be just as harmful as punches."

SACRIFICED TO THE DRAGON

"Neil was a right bastard. I sure hope you're not comparing him to me."

Bram was quiet for a second before he said, "If you keep focusing your hatred of humans on Melanie, then you could end up being worse. I had put my hope into Neil changing because of the clan depending on him. I failed and will always have to live with that, but I'm not about to watch one of my dragon-shifters sentence another human female into a life of misery."

Tristan was thinking of how to respond to that when he noticed Samira's entrance at the far door. Since Melanie was a few inches shorter, he couldn't see her brown hair with all of the tall dragon-shifters in the way. His dragon urged him to go find her, but as he battled the beast for control, the crowd parted to reveal Melanie.

He almost didn't recognize her. Her long hair was swept up atop her head, with strategic tendrils dangling near her ears. The light green material of the dress set off her eyes and made her creamy, bared skin glow. His gaze moved from her face and bare shoulders to the way the material hugged her breasts and ribcage before flaring out around her belly and hips. The dress was in the traditional style and tied on one side, in case a dragonwoman needed to shift, and the image of him untying the dress with his teeth and exposing her creamy, warm skin flashed into his mind.

He felt Bram's hand on his shoulder and he nearly jumped. Bram squeezed his shoulder and said, "You can stop drooling now, Tristan. Go greet your human sacrifice."

The noise had died down to a low hum. Everyone was waiting for him to introduce the new arrival.

He nodded and descended the dais. He ignored the stares of his clan and never took his gaze from his sacrifice as he approached her. While tonight was partly about introducing her

47

to the clan, it was also the time for him to stake his claim; the woman was his, at least, for the time being.

For the first time since he'd met her, Melanie looked nervous. She had her hands clasped in front of her in a near-death grip and his inner dragon wanted to come out to wrap its body protectively around hers and soothe her. Only because of years of training to contain it did he manage to convince the beast that he would take care of her.

Of course, that meant trying not to insult her.

With Bram's words about the possibility of him turning into a worse bastard than Neil, he stopped right in front of Melanie and put out a hand. He couldn't promise to behave when they were alone, but he would at least try to behave in front of his clan.

When she placed her hand on top of his, he curled his fingers around hers and said, "At least you're fashionably late."

She blinked and said, "Thank you?"

His dragon growled a little, wanting him to give her a proper compliment, but he ignored it and motioned toward the dais with his head. On the short walk up to Bram, the mixture of her feminine scent and the warmth of her skin against his palm stirred both his beast and his cock. If this is what just being beside her did to him, what would happen when he had to kiss her?

~~~

When Samira had finally ushered Melanie into the grand meeting hall, it had taken every ounce of control Mel possessed not to bolt in the other direction. Every dragon-shifter they passed stared at her, and not all of their looks were friendly; a few were downright contemptuous.

The light lunch she'd eaten during her dress fitting from hell hadn't been enough and now her stomach was twisting with both hunger and anxiety. With all that had happened to her over the last four hours, she was exhausted. Why the dragons had to have a welcoming ceremony on the same day as her arrival was beyond her. She was starting to understand how a less stubborn person could have a meltdown.

Still, she wasn't going to be that person. She kept her chin and shoulders high as people cleared a path for them. When Samira pulled her to walk beside her instead of behind her, that's when Mel finally saw Tristan and her step faltered.

He was dressed in something that looked like an old-fashioned kilt, which left his arms and most of his chest bare. His tattoo extended from his shoulder to wrap around his arm, the dark ink only highlighting the defined muscles of his bicep. He wasn't bulky like a body builder; rather, he was lean with defined muscles similar to a swimmer. Considering the amount of upper body strength required for flying, it didn't surprise her.

She had grudgingly found him attractive before, but with all of his exposed skin and the way he was dressed now, that attraction heated her entire body, including places she didn't want to be thinking about right now.

All of a sudden, she imagined tracing the outline of his tattoo before running her hand through the light spattering of dark hair on his chest. She had just started to imagine him taking off his kilt-like outfit when Samira gripped her elbow, urged her forward, and said, "He's an attractive bloke, isn't he? Break through his mistrust and stand up to him, and you might get to enjoy all that skin against yours for more than it takes to conceive a child."

Mel's cheeks flushed and for once, she refrained from saying anything. The room full of dragon-shifters watching her every move was eating away at her fortitude to be herself at all times.

Tristan descended the dais and approached, and her heart started pounding in her chest at the flicker of appreciation in his eyes. Even she was honest enough with herself to know she looked pretty damn good in this dress. Samira had outdone herself to alter and make the dress flatter her curvy figure.

She smoothed the silky material of her skirt and the act eased some of her nervous energy.

Then Tristan was in front of her and she had trouble forcing her gaze from his chest to meet his eyes. Once she did, he put out a hand and she gingerly placed hers on top. The feel of his rough skin sent a shock through her body, straight to her core.

Despite the fact he could probably smell her arousal with his super-sensitive dragon senses, all he said was, "At least you're fashionably late."

Mel blinked. She wasn't used to compliments, even half-assed ones, and especially not from Tristan. He was being almost...nice to her. She wondered what had happened between dumping her on the doorstep of the cottage and now.

Tristan guided her toward the raised dais and she noticed the clan leader watching them.

She made an effort to smile at Bram, but the combination of the heat of Tristan's skin against hers and the smell of sky and man made it hard for her to think of anything but the warm dragon-shifter at her side. Samira's words, about having his skin against hers beyond conceiving, entered her mind. She looked up at his face and wondered who this dragonman truly was. Now that she understood what humans had done to his mother, she started to see why he didn't want her. Could he ever get past that?

She would tackle his issues tomorrow. For now, she focused on maintaining her composure. Dragon-shifters were part animal. One of the few things she'd discovered in her research was that their beasts assessed new acquaintances just like animals did, and she wasn't about to give them a reason to place her low in the pecking order.

They ascended the steps and Tristan stopped them in front of Bram. The clan leader's blue eyes pierced hers, but she was prepared for it this time. She said, "Hello again."

Bram put out a hand and she placed hers on top of his. His grip was firm and solid, but she didn't get a thrill from this man's firm touch as she had with Tristan's.

The clan leader kissed her hand, and she heard a growl from behind her, not quite certain why Tristan would growl at his clan leader. Or had Melanie broken some unwritten cultural rule?

Before she could ask, Bram straightened up and released her hand. In contrast to his earlier tough, almost grumpy composure back during their meeting, a smile now tugged at his lips. He gestured with his head toward the center of the dais. "Come. Let's get the formalities over with so that we can eat and you can start to relax."

She doubted she would be able to relax for weeks, if ever, but she nodded, anxious to get this whole process over with.

Bram raised a hand and the hall fell quiet. When he spoke, his voice was loud and clear, and in English. "We are gathered here to welcome our newest female sacrifice. Her name is Melanie Hall. Tristan MacLeod has been assigned as her male. As with previous contracts, we have guaranteed her safety for the next six months. Each and every one of us will do whatever it takes to protect her."

A few people muttered words she couldn't understand, but as Bram scanned the room, the hall went deadly quiet again.

Bram continued, "Per tradition, we'll now finalize Tristan's claim on the sacrifice with the First Kiss."

She blinked. A first kiss? Here, in front of all these people?

Bram turned toward her and Melanie forced her gaze from the crowd of people to Bram's deep blue eyes. "You have offered yourself as a sacrifice to Clan Stonefire, and while this has been finalized on paper, it is our tradition for the male in charge of you to solidify his claim to the entire clan by kissing you in front of everyone, which will guarantee his protection." He motioned with his hand and she felt Tristan's heat beside her again. "Tristan MacLeod, is there something you'd like to ask our guest?"

She turned toward Tristan. It took everything she had to look at his eyes and not his lips.

His brown eyes were unreadable. While she wished they were full of heat in anticipation of her kiss, the sight was far better than disgust or contempt. As she waited for him to speak, her heart pounded in her chest. Would it be a mere peck or the full-on, tongue-twirling variety?

He opened his mouth to speak and she stopped breathing.

~~~

As Tristan waited for Bram to say all the necessary formalities, his inner dragon urged him to pull Melanie flush up against his body and kiss her already. The kiss did more than physically show his claim in front of the clan; it also covered the sacrifice in his scent, which would help to keep the other males away.

But Tristan was stronger than his dragon, and he maintained the distance between their bodies. If he was going to survive tasting Melanie for the first time, without taking her right there on the stage, he needed to prepare himself.

He took slow, controlled breaths and imagined scratching his dragon's nose, and then behind his ear. Before long, his inner dragon was crooning in contentment. Inside his mind, Tristan said, *You and I can have her soon. Until then, let the human part of us take care of her.*

His dragon seemed to settle, trusting Tristan at his word.

And just in time, too. Bram asked, "Tristan MacLeod, is there something you'd like to ask our guest?"

Tristan kept his features expressionless as Melanie turned toward him, her cheeks flushed. He could hear her heart racing, but the question was whether it was because she was nervous or because she was aroused at the idea of kissing him.

Rather than think on it, he said in a loud, clear voice, "Ms. Melanie Hall, will you do me the honor of allowing me to show my promise to protect you with a First Kiss?"

She swallowed, but then quickly nodded.

He took a step toward her and raised his hands to her cheeks. Melanie sucked in a breath at his touch, and he simultaneously felt a little thrill from the heat of her soft skin. Right here, right now, she looked innocent and vulnerable; nothing like the fiery woman who'd stood up to him a few hours ago.

If she were a dragon-shifter female, he'd probably kiss her and never let go.

But she was human, and he needed to be careful. He'd give her a quick peck and then somehow survive the rest of the celebration and the following day.

He gave his inner beast one last soothing sound before he stroked her cheek and lowered his head to meet her lips.

Her lips were soft, warm, and tasted of woman. The contact shot straight to his cock, and suddenly, the quick peck wasn't enough. He needed to feel the moist warmth of her mouth. His inner dragon roared that he wanted, no needed, to discover her taste.

He could've fought his beast, but with Melanie's scent surrounding him and the softness of her skin under his fingers, he couldn't make himself pull away.

Instead, Tristan traced the seam of her lips with his tongue, but she didn't open. With a growl, he moved one of his hands from her face to her waist and hauled her lush body up against his.

Melanie gasped the instant her softness came up against his hard body and he took advantage, thrusting his tongue into her mouth. Her taste was a mixture of woman and something sweet, a biscuit perhaps, and he was desperate for more. He gave one stroke, then another, learning the contours and feel of her mouth.

But as desperate as he was to taste her, she stood still, as if she was just waiting for him to hurry up and finish.

His dragon didn't like that one bit. *More. Taste. Take more.*

To please his dragon, he just needed to give her a little encouragement.

He nipped and sucked her bottom lip before moving to the top one. He pressed her soft belly harder against his aching cock and she let out a little noise of surprise. He invaded her mouth again, but as he stroked her tongue, her hand went to his shoulder and she started to meet his strokes, shyly at first, before gaining confidence.

While her belly was pressed against his cock and her taste was filling his mouth, he desperately wanted to fill his hands with some of her curves. He could think of nothing but what it would feel like to hold and caress the heavy weight of her breast in his hand. Then he could tug and roll her hard little nipple with his fingers, and eventually take the tight bud into his mouth and start his torture all over again.

His inner dragon chimed in. *Yes, we need to tease our female and ready her for our pleasure.*

He slowly started to move a hand up her ribs to put his plan in motion when someone pinched his arm. He broke the kiss with a growl, only to find Bram staring at him with a warning in his eyes. Tristan pulled Melanie tighter against his body. This was his female. His. He needed to get her away from the other males. He didn't even trust his clan leader. Any male that saw her would want her.

Tristan looked down at his female, her eyes wide, her lips red and swollen, and he moved to kiss her again. His dragon's need was pounding inside his head: *Mark her. Protect her from the other males. Make sure everyone knows she's ours.*

He had barely started stroking inside her mouth again when he felt a grip on the back of his neck and he growled louder this time as he forced his lips from the warm female to find Bram staring at him. When the clan leader whispered, "Stop it," his leader's words broke through his lust-haze. He glanced down at Melanie, her lips slightly parted and her eyes filled with desire. Then he looked out to the crowd, and realized the enormity of what he'd nearly done. He'd been so very close to fondling her breasts, or possibly more, on a stage in front of his entire clan.

Bloody hell. What was wrong with him?

If his near public indecency wasn't bad enough, his dragon was roaring for him to kiss her again and then fuck her as soon as possible so he could brand her with his scent. Bram said something, some sort of traditional words, but Tristan was losing the battle with his dragon. If he didn't leave right now, he could very well toss Melanie over his shoulder, bring her to his cottage, and fuck her with or without her consent.

No. He wasn't that type of male. He wouldn't break his contract or force someone against her will. He needed to leave.

Without a word, he rushed down the steps of the dais and pushed past his clan members until he reached the cool night air. As he struggled to keep his human side in control, he headed for the landing and take-off area. Apart from fucking Melanie, the only thing that would calm his dragon would be a long flight followed by a tough hunt.

He stripped his clothes and imagined wings sprouting from his back; as his body grew large, his hands turned into claws and talons, and his skin turned into a tough, black hide. When he was finally a fifteen-foot tall dragon, he spread his wings, used his powerful hind legs to jump, and beat his wings to take him up into the air.

Once he was high above the Stonefire community, he let his dragon mostly take over.

As he continued to beat his wings, his inner beast let out a long roar of frustration and said, *I want the human. The other males will take her in our absence. We need her. Let's go back and claim her. She is ours.*

Tristan forced his wings to keep beating, making sure their flightpath took them away from the great hall. *But if we return, we'll*

56

miss the fat bucks I wanted to hunt. Fresh meat will help you forget about the female. Now is the only time we can go.

His dragon remained silent for a second before he said, *Yes, let's hunt. It will give us more energy to claim our female.*

Not wishing to debate the finer points of when or how they'd claim Melanie Hall, Tristan said, *Right, then let's go.*

Changing their direction slightly, Tristan headed for their favorite hunting spot in northern England.

As the tension started to ease from his body, the human-half of Tristan started to realize he was fucked. His dragon's possessiveness wasn't normal. The only time a dragon would get so out of control was when they'd tasted their potential mate.

And Tristan's dragon-half wanted a human named Melanie Hall.

CHAPTER SIX

One second, Melanie Hall had been enjoying the most passionate kiss of her life in Tristan's arms full of tongue, teeth, and delicious friction of lips. And the next, he'd pushed her away and bolted from the hall without so much as a word or even a backward glance.

She watched in confusion as Tristan exited the building. Was this part of the normal First Kiss ceremony? Or had something gone wrong? She absolutely hated not knowing what was going on around her.

Once Tristan was gone, everyone turned around to stare at her. Some were whispering while others were shaking their heads. She had no idea if Tristan's actions were normal or not, but clearly the dragon-shifters knew something she didn't.

She focused on that, trying to find out what they knew, to keep her hurt from showing. She'd never been kissed like that before, as if Tristan had been starving and she was the only thing that could ease his hunger. Yet, at the end, Tristan hadn't been able to get away from her fast enough.

She felt Bram's hand on her arm and she looked up at him. His expression was guarded when he said, "Come. Sit down with me, Melanie."

His voice broke through her shock and despite her resolve to stay strong, her voice cracked. "I don't understand. What just happened?"

He gestured toward the table. "Sit down with me and I'll explain as much as I can."

She nodded and somehow made her legs carry her to the seat next to Bram. The table faced out, and she could still see all of the Stonefire dragons looking at her. Now that she'd seen the dragon-shifter females, who were all tall, toned, and beautiful, she wondered if the whispers were about Tristan's misfortune to be assigned her, a mere human.

No. As humiliating as Tristan pushing her away after their kiss and fleeing was, she wasn't going to give everyone the satisfaction of dismissing her because she was curvy, short, and a "mere human".

She took a deep breath and exhaled. She did it one more time and decided she had her emotions under control enough to talk without breaking down. She looked over at Bram. "Tell me why they're all whispering and staring at me. Since Tristan isn't here to protect me, it's your job now to do it."

He gave a half smile. "Never give up that backbone or core of steel, lass. It's sure to win you the respect of the clan."

She wasn't sure how to interpret the pseudo-compliment, so she decided to press her question again. "Just tell me. Please. Is that how it always goes with the human sacrifices?"

Bram shook his head. "No, we haven't seen anything like it since Samira."

She frowned. "Samira? What does she have to do with this?"

"I wish I could tell you it's nothing and that everything will be fine. But in reality, things could go very, very wrong if we're not careful."

She didn't like the sound of that. "You aren't making any sense. Please just tell me what's going on."

Bram gave her a serious look. "Tristan's dragon-half wants you as its mate."

She blinked. "What? Dragon mates are like spouses, right?" Bram nodded. "Then how in the world could his dragon want me for that kind of future? I've barely known Tristan a day."

"That doesn't matter. As soon as a dragon-shifter kisses a potential mate, the dragon knows what the human-half ignores. Mainly, that you are his or her best chance at not only reproducing several times, but also that you're his or her best chance at happiness, which means a long life and the ability to raise young."

Melanie frowned. Despite her best attempt at researching the dragon-shifters before coming here, all of this information was new to her. "From one kiss, his inner dragon knows all of this? But how?"

"Not even we understand everything about our dragons. But if nothing else, our inner beasts rely on instinct. It could be something about your scent or the build of your body that draws the dragon. All I know is that I've never seen a dragon act so possessively during a First Kiss without that dragon going on to try to claim the person in question. The same reaction happened when Samira's mate, Liam, kissed her on this same stage, almost four years ago."

She took another deep breath. This was too much to process right now; she'd have to sort it all out more carefully later. In the meantime, she was going to use this opportunity to get more information on the dragon mate business. "Okay, let's pretend I accept all of this for the moment. Why would this put me in danger? If his dragon wants me as a mate, I would think that Tristan's inner dragon would want to protect me, not harm me."

Bram shook his head. "Not necessarily. We may look human, but our dragons are primal and take what they want. If Tristan loses the battle with his dragon-half, he could very well take you against your will and keep taking you until he can scent you're carrying his child."

Someone put a dish of food in front of her, but Melanie was no longer hungry. "Is there a way to stop him? After all, you said 'potential mate', which means it doesn't always succeed."

Bram's mouth turned grim. "A dragon will only move on in two instances. First, if either party dies. Second, after a child is born. In the latter case, the dragon is satisfied with an offspring to care for and is willing to try again with someone else if the female doesn't want him."

So much for finding a way to keep the sex-crazed dragonman from chasing her or for transferring her sacrifice contract to another dragon-shifter male. She had a feeling that if Tristan's dragon-half was determined to have her, no other male would be stupid enough to stand in the way.

She was stuck with him. "And neither of those two cases qualifies right now, right?"

"No. At this point, the best thing is for you to allow him to take you early. Otherwise, we'll have to drug him unconscious until the third day, when the contract allows him to touch you. And even then, while human Tristan would wait for your consent if you weren't ready by the third day, the dragon-half probably won't."

Melanie noticed the water glass in front of her and started tracing shapes in the condensation with her finger. The action helped her to remain calm and resist letting her emotions break free.

So much for trying to get to know both Tristan and his clan tomorrow. Bram was suggesting for her to jump into bed with Tristan blind. Yes, although she was attracted to him, could she do it? Could she allow a man she barely knew, and who had treated her badly except for a short period this evening, to have sex with her?

She wasn't completely terrified of the idea, but she wanted more information. "How long do we have before he returns?"

"I'd wager he went for a hunt, and he should be out until mid-morning tomorrow. Our dragons always like to sleep in dragon form on a full belly, and they can be lazy bastards when they choose."

She had a feeling Bram was trying to lighten the mood a little, but it wasn't working. "Let's say I agree, and I have sex with Tristan early and he keeps at it until I'm pregnant. Then what? I know he doesn't like humans. Will he just closet me away until I birth his child and then toss me aside?"

"Since I've never fallen prey to a dragon mate frenzy before, I don't know. I think it's best you talk to Samira. She's the only human female we have here who has both experienced the frenzy and accepted a dragon-shifter's claim."

Mel nodded. From what little she knew of Samira, the woman was happy. That gave Mel a small hope that things might not be as bad as her gut was telling her they were going to be.

Bram signaled for one of his men to come to their table. After he whispered an order, he stood and offered his hand to her. "Will you allow me to see you safe to your cottage? If I'm by your side, the others won't start pestering you with questions. And since I just sent for Samira to meet you at your cottage for a chat, I think you want to get there as soon as possible."

Mel placed her hand in his and straightened her shoulders. The memory of Tristan's kiss, his act of leaving her, and the whole news of a dragon's mate frenzy was starting to sink in and it was overwhelming. She needed to find somewhere private to process everything that had happened to her in the last twenty minutes. As it was, she was on the verge of an information overload-related breakdown. Nevertheless, she was half-British. She could keep a stiff upper lip like the best of them and contain her emotions for a little bit longer.

As Bram maneuvered her down the stairs and through the crowd, she kept her gaze fixed ahead on nothing in particular. She just needed to make it to her cottage, and then she could change her clothes and try to figure out what to do from here.

Thirty minutes later, Melanie was curled up on the couch in her cottage trying not to cry. Despite changing into her favorite cotton pajamas and taking out all the pins in her hair, relaxed was the last word she'd use to describe her situation. All she could think about was how a half-crazed dragonman wanted to fuck her until she was pregnant.

Yes, "fucking her" was the appropriate phrase to use. She could hardly call a dragonman crazy with lust thrusting into her until she collapsed or conceived as doing anything else. It certainly wouldn't be making love.

She squeezed the pillow in her arms for comfort. She'd never expected a fairy tale ending by coming here, but at the very least, she'd wanted a day to get to know Tristan before getting naked with him. She'd spent more time with the single one-night stand she'd had during her undergraduate years than she had with the dragonman who intended for her to bear his child.

Now more than ever, she wished some of these practices had shown up in her research. Of course, she could understand why the dragon-shifters kept the mate frenzy a secret. It would deter a large number of women from ever signing up to be sacrifices, and considering the uneven birth rates of thirty-five percent female to sixty-five percent male amongst the dragon-shifters, they needed human women if their race was to survive.

The fact that dragon-shifters needed humans to survive was ironic considering the humans were the ones who had decimated their numbers in the first place.

There was a knock on the door. Melanie tossed aside her pillow and jumped up to answer it. She desperately needed a distraction.

She opened the door a crack, but it was Samira, so she opened the door wide. She tried to smile, but failed, and tears started to roll down her cheeks. She didn't want to cry, but she couldn't help it. Losing her family, being thrust into a new culture she didn't understand, and finally, being the object of a dragon's frenzy despite the fact he hated her was enough to make even the strongest person break down.

Samira put an arm around her shoulders, closed the door, and guided them toward the couch. Once they sat down, she said, "There, there, dear. I know it sounds scary, but it doesn't have to be. Dragonmen in a frenzy can be overpowering and passionate, but they will also protect you with their life."

Mel managed to blink back her tears and wiped her hands across her eyes. "That doesn't sound like what Bram told me."

Samira tsked. "Of course not. His dragon has never experienced a mate frenzy, and he thinks humans are too fragile to survive it. Yet dragonwomen deal with the frenzies when they happen without a problem. They're quite rare, you know, the mate frenzies."

"Maybe so, but at least the dragonwomen know what to expect."

Samira took Mel's chin in her hand and forced her to look at her. "Listen to me. Imagine the best sex of your life with the hottest man you've ever known. Not only that, but a man who turns into a fierce protector type of father from the second his child is born. That is what you get with a mate-frenzied male. Tristan may fight it at first, but he's not intentionally cruel. After all, he trains the young dragons. I had wanted you to see him in action with the children tomorrow, but it looks like you might not get the chance to see him in his teacher role for quite a while."

"A teacher? Tristan?"

Samira nodded. "It's one of the hardest jobs in the clan to teach young dragons how to control their beasts as well as to fly and hunt without breaking the law. But Tristan has done it with ease for the past twelve years."

The image of Tristan being patient or kind with anyone was foreign to her. "I just wish I could see that side of him first."

Samira's face softened. "I saw the way you looked at him back in the main hall, and I know you're attracted to him. Is it really so bad to have sex with him a day early? The sooner you're pregnant, the sooner you can get to know the real Tristan and not his half-crazed dragon."

If she were honest with herself, Mel didn't think the sex would be that bad. However, a small part of her had wanted Tristan to get to know her without being forced to do so because she was carrying his child. Especially since once she was pregnant, there was a high chance she might not live past the birth.

There was another thing for her to worry about; she could die in less than a year.

Speaking of pregnant women, she remembered Caitriona and her aura of defeat. "Did Cait's male succumb to the frenzy, too?"

"No. Neil only did his duty and impregnated her before he screwed everything up. He was a selfish asshole with no sense of honor."

She wanted to ask why he'd been assigned a human sacrifice in the first place, but Mel decided to focus on her fast-approaching fate. After all, Tristan should be back in less than twelve hours. "So you and your mate are the only ones who've experienced this before?"

Samira shook her head. "No. There is a dragonwoman paired with a dragonman. It's not just a human-dragon-shifter thing. It's probably impossible to set up a meeting tonight, but I'm sure either I or Bram can set up a meeting with them in time."

She turned to face Samira. "Tell me, did you sleep with your mate before you knew him, too?"

Samira smiled. "I spent maybe an hour more in his company than you have with Tristan by this point. But yes, I slept with him the very first night, after Bram and Ella, the female dragon-shifter who also went through the mate frenzy, talked with me. Liam is kind to everyone from the start, whereas Tristan takes some time to open up, which made things a little easier on my end. I was scared for about two minutes before Liam made a joke and I soon forgot about anything except his hot, naked body over mine."

She did remember Tristan's toned chest and arms from back in the hall, and how it'd felt to be pressed up against his hard body. She would be lying if she didn't say she wanted to feel his heat pressed up against her skin again, such as with the rough hair on his chest rubbing against her bared breasts. Or to feel his rough hands caressing the soft skin of her hip.

She nearly blinked at the sex fantasy that had started to play out in her mind. It seemed that talking with Samira was helping to calm her nerves. Mel realized she'd only been afraid and crying because she'd had no idea of what to expect. But it was starting to sound less like a nightmare and more like hot sex with a stranger.

She was very close to saying screw it and just let Tristan have her. But before she could take the last step to acceptance and vocalize her thoughts, Samira spoke again. "The decision is up to you. But if you think you can't do it, then you can come stay with me. Liam, my mate, has already said he'd gather his brothers, sister, and his friends to protect you from Tristan until the third day." She took and squeezed Mel's hand. "Just tell me what you plan to do."

She stared into Samira's deep brown eyes and decided that she'd made an ally who might turn into her friend. Mel hadn't been sure at first if they'd get along since Samira had seemed to dismiss Cait's depressed state. Now, after the woman was all but saying she'd chase off a crazy dragon just to help her, Mel decided she'd been wrong about her. No doubt, there were things about Cait that Mel didn't know. Samira could just be acting as the other human woman had asked.

She took Samira's hand in hers and squeezed. "Thank you for the offer, but no. As soon as Tristan is back, he should come here and I'll start doing what I was brought here to do—have sex with a dragon-shifter."

CHAPTER SEVEN

Tristan had resisted the pull to return to Melanie for as long as he could. The hunt, taking down two bucks, and the resulting sleep had preoccupied his dragon-half for a little over half a day. Now the dragon was overpowering him little by little, and he knew that it was better to track down Melanie with his human-half marginally in charge rather than with his dragon in complete control.

Especially since he knew full well his dragon wouldn't bother with consent, and human or not, Melanie didn't deserve that.

Female. Home. Now.

Still in dragon form, he jumped up and beat his wings until he was high enough to use the wind currents to glide toward Stonefire's land. He trusted that Bram had prepared Melanie for what was about to happen. Otherwise, he would face the ultimate test of control once he landed back home.

As he soared south, he placated his dragon with thoughts about Melanie's soft, warm body pressed up against him. Or how her mouth had felt like silk against his tongue. His dragon hummed in appreciation and pressed Tristan to fly faster. The dragon wanted to see the human's curves in the flesh.

His dragon was a persistent bastard, but one of the upsides of having a dragon-half was that it would give him incredible stamina, allowing him to fuck Melanie for as long as it took to impregnate her. Once that was done, he could go back to his life and not be faced with seeing the human on a daily basis. Provided, of course, he could prevent his dragon from forming a long-lasting attachment.

While he'd keep Melanie at arm's length once she was pregnant, he wouldn't be as harsh as Neil had been with Cait; he would avoid insulting his human and would always protect Melanie and his unborn child against any threat. But Tristan wanted to prevent his inner beast from forming too much of an attachment to Melanie because the mate claim frenzy was dangerous. The more his dragon grew attached, the less his human-half would be able to deny his beast. His honor and duty would prevent harming the human, but there was no way in hell he wanted to be mated to one for the rest of his life.

His sister was still suffering years later because of the damage caused by humans and their greed.

Soon, he was gliding down to the landing area inside Stonefire. Once he was on solid ground again, his inner beast roared. His female was here, and she was fertile. They needed to find her. Other males might already be trying to take her.

Tristan reassured his beast they would find her, but first, they needed to be in human form.

His dragon retreated a little, and Tristan imagined his wings retreating into his back, his forelegs straightening, his talons turning into fingers, and his stature shrinking back to his six-foot-three height. The pain of the shift and change of his body was as natural to him as breathing, and within a few seconds, he was in human form again, naked as the day he was born.

A male approached him and his dragon sneered, but soon calmed down. He was the only male who could deal with him right now and not end up a bloody mess on the ground. Bram was clan leader; even his dragon deferred to Bram's position and slightly greater dominance.

When his clan leader reached him, Bram's expression was unreadable. "Are you under control?"

His dragon paced inside his head and said, *Our female is waiting. Why are we stopping? Can't our leader see how much we need our female? She will give us young, which will help the clan. We should go. Now.*

Soon, he told his dragon. It didn't really calm the beast, but allowed Tristan enough control to answer Bram coherently. "Barely. Is Melanie ready? And make it quick, Bram. I don't want to lose complete control of my beast."

"She's ready and willing. Still, all I ask is to keep your human-half in control for as long as you can. While Samira talked to her, I don't know if Melanie truly understands what's about to happen to her."

His dragon growled. *Our female is waiting. Go to her. Now!*

Tristan grit his teeth, fighting the urge to leave. "You know I'll try. But I need to go before it's too late."

Bram nodded. "Come see me when it's done."

He nodded and half-jogged toward Melanie's cottage. His beast kept repeating, *"Female. Now. Hurry."* over and over inside his head.

He reached her cottage and with incredible effort, he managed to stop at the door and knock. His dragon roared, but Tristan said to his beast, *Wait a bloody second.*

Thankfully, the door opened. Melanie stood before him in a fluffy white bathrobe. Her eyes widened. "Oh. It's you."

Now. Now. Now. She is fertile. We must fuck her.

SACRIFICED TO THE DRAGON

Not yet. Tristan said through gritted teeth, "You've been told what will happen. I'm not sure how much longer I can keep my dominance over my dragon. I need to know: Are you willing?"

Her eyes were a mixture of emotions, but he was too far gone to recognize what they were. He barely heard her reply when she said, "Yes."

"Thank fuck." He rushed at her, tossed her over his shoulder, shut the door, and made a beeline for the bed. He tossed her down and her robe fell open to reveal a silky blue nightie that barely covered her tits and pussy.

Ours. Take her. Now.

Tristan listened to his dragon and covered her soft body with his naked one. He would explore her warm, womanly curves later. For now, he reached between her legs and ran a finger through her slit. She was wet and swollen for him, and his hard cock went even harder.

He ripped her nightie to pieces and grabbed one of her lush, ample breasts, rolling her nipple to a hard point. When she let out a moan, he was at his limit. Tristan positioned his cock and thrust into her in one, swift motion.

At the feel of her warm, tight pussy around his dick, his dragon hummed. *Yes. She is our female. It's time to make her understand that.*

But his human-half was in enough control to lean down and kiss her first. He pushed his tongue into her sweet, warm mouth, exploring every inch. He started to move his hips and the human moaned into his mouth before he felt her hands on his shoulders.

He ran his hands down her soft sides until he reached her wide hips. He tightened his hold so she would stay in place as he started to pound harder. In and out. Flesh slapped against flesh.

Female. Ours. Take her. Harder.

But it wasn't rough enough for his beast. The dragon wanted to own the female's pussy; let her know she belonged to him.

To please his dragon and do exactly that, he broke their kiss. When he looked into Melanie's green eyes, the lust and desire there shot straight to his balls.

His human and dragon halves growled in unison and he tightened his grip on her hips. The need to fill her with his seed was overwhelming. Without it, she couldn't bear his young. And his dragon wanted this female to bear its young.

He moved faster and faster until the pressure built, and with a few more quick thrusts, he stilled as his dick spent inside of her, each spurt and spasm giving him a higher chance to impregnate her and prevent the other males from stealing her away. While she carried his child, his scent would be branded into her skin.

As he finished, the chemicals of his semen caused Melanie to cry out in orgasm. His dragon hummed, urging him to flip her over and take her all over again from behind.

Our female. Again. Fuck her.

His human-half was still in control by a thread, and Tristan moved to Melanie's breast, aching to taste her hard, pink nipple before the dragon took over and thought of nothing but fucking the female until she carried their young.

~~~

Melanie had expected Tristan to show up on her doorstep, but she hadn't been prepared for the way he'd tossed her on the bed, ripped her clothes, and started pounding into her like nothing else mattered.

Just the sight of his naked body and hard cock when she'd answered the door had sent wetness rushing through her legs. Him tossing her over his shoulder and pressing her breasts and nipples against his back had only aroused her further. So when he thrust his thick, long cock into her, it slid right in, filling her in a way she'd never felt before; full to the point of almost pain.

He was rough and demanding as he fucked her, but the sensations of his hard cock inside her, his tongue twining with hers, and his rough hands gripping the skin of her hips made her forget about anything but the pleasure.

Then, as he stilled, she actually felt each hot spurt of semen inside her, quickly followed by the most intense orgasm of her life.

She didn't know how long she'd been spasming with lights dancing before her eyes before she felt a wet, hot mouth on her right breast. Tristan teased her nipple with his teeth before sucking it deep in his mouth and swirling the tight bud with his tongue. She let out a cry and raised a hand to his head, threading her fingers through his thick, dark hair. She murmured, "Tristan."

At his name, he released her nipple with a pop and looked up at her. His pupils flashed to slits before returning to round; the dragon was close to the surface. In a growly voice, he said, "Again."

Since any man she'd been with before had needed time to recover before going another round, she said, "More sex? Already?"

He nodded as he palmed her breasts and squeezed. Since they were already heavy with desire, the pressure of his fingers on her tender flesh sent a shock to straight between her legs.

She should be sore and tired, but she felt surprisingly full of energy. And a small part of her wondered what the dragonman would do next. His need to mate must be rubbing off on her; she was hornier than she'd ever been in her life.

She said, "I'm willing, Tristan. Take me again."

He growled and leaned back on his heels. His posture gave her a chance to stare at his thick, still hard cock. How all those inches had fit into her in the first place, she didn't know. However, for reasons she couldn't explain, she desperately wanted—no, needed—to feel it inside her again.

Tristan growled, and between one second and the next, he flipped her over on the mattress. His hands caressed her large, squishy buttocks. His touch was rough and warm, and each slow brush of his fingers was deliberate and made her feel treasured and desired.

She knew most men liked a big ass to go from behind since it gave them a cushion, but Tristan's caresses made her feel like he'd been waiting for an ass like hers his entire life.

Then his hands reached beneath her hips and pulled up her body until she was on her knees with her ass in the air. She refrained from asking questions since Samira had told her that when the dragon was mostly in command, it rarely replied. The inner beast was all about instinct and sensation.

Speaking of which, Tristan ran a finger through her folds and she arched into his touch with a moan, the roughness of his fingers causing a wonderful sensation along her slit. She was rewarded with a slap on her left cheek. The slight stinging pain sent more wetness between her thighs.

Tristan ran his fingers up her folds and circled her clit repeatedly. The almost-touch made her nerves throb and ache. To try to relieve it, she moved her body to try to catch his fingers on her clit. But Tristan's reflexes were faster, and he moved out of the way. She decided to try another tactic to relieve her frustration. She whimpered and wiggled her rear end.

He rewarded her with a pinch to her clit and she cried out. But before there was enough pressure to give her an orgasm, he released her.

She ached to the point of pain. If he didn't fuck her soon, she felt as if she'd burst. She whispered, "Please."

He slapped her other ass cheek. "Female. Ready. Now."

"Yes."

And without preamble, he thrust into her with one swift motion. She fisted the sheets in her hands at the intrusion. In this position, the fullness was almost too much to handle.

Then he started to move. His hands were now on her hips, guiding her forward and back against his cock, his rhythm picking up pace until his balls were slapping against her clit with each thrust.

If she'd thought he'd taken her rough before, then now he was downright brutal. He was in complete control of their rhythm and the movement of her hips, but she loved the feel of his hairy legs against hers, the pure male dominance of his touch as he pulled and pushed her hips against his. She would be bruised later, but right here, right now, she didn't care about anything but her next orgasm.

For a second, she wondered what had happened to her; she wasn't this sensual, demanding creature. Then Tristan slapped her right ass cheek and she moaned, gripping the sheets tighter in her fists. She was so close.

Tristan let out a roar as he stopped pounding and held her firmly against his cock. Again, she felt the heat of his seed and she was blinded by another intense orgasm. If Tristan hadn't been holding her up by her hips, she'd have fallen over.

Then all too soon, Tristan pulled out and she felt empty again. She must've made a noise, because Tristan flipped her on her back and said, "Again. Now."

His pupils were flashing between slits and round globes. The dragon was insatiable.

And yet, despite how exhausted she should be feeling after two wild bouts of sex, her core throbbed, wanting more.

Then Melanie did something she'd never done with a man before, and bent her legs up before running a hand to her clit. As she stroked it, she purred, "Yes. Again."

Without warning, Tristan pushed her legs wider and thrust into her again. Somewhere in the back of Melanie's mind, she wondered if she could be killed by too much sex because it was certainly looking like that might happen.

CHAPTER EIGHT

"Melanie, wake up."

Melanie turned her head into her pillow. "I'm tired. Go away."

Someone shook her shoulder. "Melanie."

She was awake enough now to realize it was a female voice speaking to her, which meant it wasn't Tristan-slash-dragon waking her up for more sex. She peeked open an eye and saw it was Samira.

She was beyond exhausted, and not to mention sore, but somehow her brain realized that the presence of someone other than Tristan in her cottage was significant. She turned her head a little and asked, "What?"

Samira brushed Melanie's hair off her face. "How're you feeling, my dear?"

She grumbled. "That is what you woke me up for?"

"No. But I need to make sure you're awake before I tell you why I'm here."

She was naked, but under a sheet, so Mel turned onto her back and stretched her arms. She grimaced at the soreness between her legs. "How long was I locked up in here?"

"A week."

Wow, a week. She vaguely remembered the sun coming and going, but it was a haze of sleeping, eating, and fucking. Oh, and orgasming. There had been lots of orgasming.

She looked over to the other side of the bed, but it was empty. While she'd done very little talking with Tristan over the last week, she'd grown used to his heat and weight either beside her or on top of her. His absence felt...wrong.

She looked back over at Samira. "Where's Tristan?"

Samira's face went expressionless. "He went back to his job this morning."

"Training the young dragons?"

Samira nodded. Melanie's brain was almost fully alert now, and she made the connection. She looked down at her belly. "That means I'm pregnant."

"Yes. He told Bram that your scent changed last night. When you carry a dragon-shifter's child, you also carry the father's scent. At least until the child is born."

I'm going to have a baby. Mel closed her eyes. Fear, relief, longing, loneliness, and even a little bit of joy swirled around inside her head. She'd known this was coming, but still, it was a shock all the same.

Especially since her baby might end up killing her in about nine months.

She took a few deep breaths. She vaguely recalled Bram telling her that when a dragon went into the mate frenzy it was because the female in question was his best chance at having children and finding happiness. Maybe, just maybe, that gave her better odds at surviving the birth.

She opened her eyes and stared at Tristan's side of the bed. While she still barely knew him since he'd been distant any time his dragon hadn't been in the forefront, the thought of growing and birthing a child by herself, amongst strangers no less, brought tears to her eyes.

Mel felt a hand on her shoulder and she turned her head. Samira gave her shoulder a squeeze and said, "Don't worry, Mel. Until Tristan realizes he's a fool for staying away from you, you can come stay with me and Liam."

She blinked back her tears. Having someone nearby who'd gone through this whole process before made her feel better. "Thanks."

Samira gave another squeeze before she stood up. "I'll draw you a bath and then make you something to eat. After that, we'll pack your things and you can move in with me tonight."

Too tired and full of emotion, Mel merely nodded again and watched Samira head into the bathroom.

As the sound of running water filled the room, Mel curled onto her side and put her hands under her pillow. Conceiving had been her entire reason for coming here, and expecting anything more than that was foolish. But somewhere deep inside, she'd believed that Tristan wouldn't just knock her up and leave without so much as a glance.

But he had.

She almost started crying but then her stomach rumbled. Mel decided it was more important to focus on getting clean and feeding herself than crying tears over the dragon-shifter male she'd been assigned. She wasn't the type of person to wallow in self-pity, and starting tomorrow, she was going to distract herself by exploring the dragon-shifters' community and learning about their culture. Just because she was pregnant didn't mean she was incapacitated. She fully intended to carry out her plan and find something to write about for her doctoral thesis.

"Mel, the bath's ready!"

Uncaring about her nakedness, Mel climbed out of bed and went to take a bath. Maybe once she washed off Tristan's scent she could stop thinking about his kisses. Or his caresses. Or the way he'd made her feel like the most beautiful woman in the world.

After all, he'd only done those things because of his dragon. The man was consumed with so much hate for humans that he would abandon her without a word the instant he'd fulfilled his end of the contract and had known she was with child.

If that's how he wanted things to be, then so be it. Bram had said a woman could refuse the mate claim after a child was born. In nine months' time, Mel would be both a mother and free of a man who wanted nothing to do with her.

~~~

Tristan watched as two seven-year-olds squeezed their eyes shut and tried to shift. One managed to turn a hand into a claw with talons, but only for a few seconds before it morphed back into a human hand. The second child succeeded in turning a patch of his skin on his neck deep red, which would be the color of his hide, before that also disappeared.

He whistled between his teeth at the two children and they opened their eyes. He said, "That's a good start, but if you're not working with your dragon, you'll never be able to change and maintain the shape."

The little female looked up at him with big, brown eyes and said, "But Mr. MacLeod, I am working with my dragon. I pet her and coax her, but it doesn't seem to work."

Since he'd been doing this for years, he resisted a smile at the little one's innocence. "Right now, your dragon is young and she wants you to pamper her. But, Misa, your dragon will soon become a strong beast that will fight for control. No matter how much your dragon begs or pleads, you must learn to be the one in command. Only then will you be able to channel your inner beast and make the change into a full-fledged dragon in the flesh. Does that make sense?"

Misa nodded and Tristan looked to the lad. "Were you doing the same thing?" The boy looked sheepish, but nodded. Tristan pointed to the far corner of the clearing encircled by high rock formations that served as his outdoor classroom. "Take some time to get a grip on your dragons. In a little while, I'll call you over and we'll try again. Okay?"

The two young nodded and scurried to the far side. Since all ten of today's pupils were attempting their first shift or, like the two students he'd just dismissed, were getting to know their dragons, he had nothing to distract him from Melanie, let alone from thinking about his unborn child.

If everything went according to plan, he was going to be a father.

When he'd first scented the change, joy had shot through his body. The new life would not only add to his clan, it might give him and his sister the new start they desperately needed.

But the scent had also made his dragon go from being slightly possessive of Melanie to downright domineering. Despite everything, he'd tried to keep his beast from forming a bond, yet the dragon had become attached.

And so, when Tristan had been in control of his dragon again early this morning, he'd left without a word and returned to his duties. Working with the young dragon-shifters was the only way to force his beast to be calm and collected; protecting his clan's young was the highest instinctual priority. Hell, working with and overseeing the children were the only things he could do to both stay away from Melanie and please his dragon.

As he walked around, checking his pupils' progress, his mind started to wander to the last week. The first day had been all about letting his dragon loose to fuck the shit out of the human, but as the week progressed, and not even his mate frenzy induced energy-giving semen could prevent the human's exhaustion, he'd had to let her rest more and more often. When Melanie had curled against him in her sleep, he hadn't had the heart to push her away. And before long, holding Melanie's soft, plump body in his arms had become something he'd looked forward to.

He'd very nearly forgotten that she was human.

Some might say he was crazy for focusing his hatred on a random human female, but apart from the dips and curves of her body or her soft cries during an orgasm, he knew very little about her. He wasn't going to let his dick overrule his brain on this.

He'd hide out with the young dragon-shifters for a few days. He hoped the distance would help lessen his dragon's attachment and need to claim her for good. Once that was done, he could check on the future mother of his child and investigate if she was a threat to his clan.

And if she was, mother of his child or not, he would find a way to get rid of her after their child was born.

~~~

Two days full of rest with food and sleep had done wonders for Melanie's mental state. She no longer felt like crying every two seconds, and her brain was working at full power again, which was great since Bram had asked to see her.

Since the asshole, her current codename for Tristan, hadn't bothered to even stop by and say hi, she was going to turn to her other designated protector and find out what she was actually allowed to do here. If she had to spend nine months twiddling her thumbs, she'd go insane.

She passed an unknown female dragon-shifter and Melanie smiled in greeting. But the woman glared at her and hissed, "You shouldn't be here, you human whore."

She blinked. After spending so much time with Samira, she'd forgotten that not everyone accepted her presence here.

Before she could say anything in response, the dragonwoman was gone.

She instinctively put a hand over her belly. Liam had picked up Mel's "scent of pregnancy" yesterday within seconds of entering his and Samira's home. While she had yet to take any official pregnancy test, two dragon-shifters scenting it had made the whole thing a lot more real to her. Now that she had something to protect, she really needed to get to know the people of this community and weed out the threats from the allies.

She may not be a dragon, but she'd do anything to protect her family.

But since she couldn't even go around Stonefire's community without Bram's say-so, she picked up her pace. She needed to convince Stonefire's leader that she wasn't a threat. Well, as long as no one threatened her, of course. She wasn't about to take people's crap just to keep the peace. Even if the asshole who'd knocked her up wasn't going to protect her, Liam and his brothers and sister would. Liam was an actual nice guy, and for a second, Melanie had been jealous of Samira.

Then the jealousy had passed. Nice was a little too boring for her taste.

She nearly faltered at that thought. What? Did she prefer a broody, asshole of a sex god instead?

She shook her head and sprinted the last few feet to Bram's office. She needed a distraction.

When she knocked, she was told to enter. Inside, Bram was at his desk. He gestured toward the chair. After she sat down, he took a deep inhalation and said, "It's true, then, about the baby. You're well, I take it?"

She resisted being snarky since this man was the key to any sort of freedom she might have here. "As well as anyone in my situation could be."

He nodded. "Good. While I wanted to see how you're doing, the real reason I asked to see you is because I have a job for you."

"A job?"

"Yes. Two, in fact. The first is more of a personal favor than anything, but I'm hoping you can help me out."

Doing a favor might help her in the long run. "What do you need?"

"It's about Cait."

She leaned forward in her chair. "What happened? Is she okay? I wanted to check on her, but I was told I had to come here first."

Bram stared at her for a second then said, "Before Tristan's mate frenzy came on, you met with Cait. You know she's had a tough time here, and it's mostly my fault." When she didn't countermand him, he gave a sardonic smile. "Okay, it's ninety-nine percent my fault she's miserable. I never should have made Neil take a sacrifice. But it's done and can't be changed." He leaned back in his chair. "You know she's depressed and unhappy. What you might not know is that after talking with you the first day before the welcoming ceremony, she actually started venturing outside her cottage. Only short trips, mostly to watch some of the young play in the designated safe area, but she hasn't done more than visit the healer for months now."

Now, more than ever, she wanted to check on Cait. The woman sounded lonely. But Bram had yet to ask her for the favor. "And what does this have to do with me?"

"She has about three months before she's due to give birth. I want you to be friends with her and see if she can be even marginally happy. She doesn't like Samira because Samira has a dragon male who loves her. And even though I have moved her into a cottage next to mine and have tried to take care of her ever since Neil left, she's afraid of all dragon-shifters, except maybe the children. Even though she intends to leave as soon as the child is born, I'd really like her to go back to her people as unbroken as possible."

"Why? To protect your reputation?"

"No, because it breaks my heart that she's been hurt because of me."

Bram's expression and tone made it seem as if he truly cared for Cait, but she didn't know him well enough to know if it was all an act or not. And while she'd planned on trying to befriend Cait anyway, her gut told her that this was her chance to ask for what she wanted. "I'll say yes on one condition."

He raised an eyebrow. "You want to bargain with me?" She nodded. "Not many here would try to do that. There's hope for you yet."

She didn't know how to interpret that, so she pushed on. "I want the ability to roam Stonefire's land without needing your or some other dragon-shifter's permission every time I go out."

"Do you think that wise? While no one in the clan will physically harm you, especially now that you're carrying Tristan's child, I can't control their likes or dislikes. Some of them will outright hate you for your intrusion here, and won't be afraid to show it."

Mel thought of the dragonwoman she'd encountered on the way here. "I'd rather take my chances. A few harsh words I can handle, but endless months of boredom I cannot."

"There are a few sections which will remain off limits until I can better assess your loyalties. But provided you do the second thing I ask, I don't see you roaming the unrestricted areas as a problem."

Considering she'd been here just over a week, his caveats seemed reasonable. "Okay, so what's the second thing you want to ask me for?"

"I want you to help teach the young dragons about humans."

She frowned. "About what, exactly? I'm not a trained teacher. I'm studying to be an anthropologist."

"I know that, and I think your degree will help you to present your people in an unbiased light. Isn't that one of the tenants of anthropology? To try and limit personal bias?"

She decided to avoid getting into complicated theory about whether that was possible or not and simply said, "For the most part, yes."

"Good. Then you're exactly what they need. Our texts are outdated, and most of my clan is still somewhat biased against your kind due to our bloody, and often violent, past. You'll be able to answer the children's questions without peppering it with hate."

She eyed Bram for a second. "Why are you so keen on changing the children's perceptions? There is still a huge amount of bias against dragon-shifters in the human world. If the children get too rosy a view, it could end up harming them in the long run."

He waved a hand in dismissal. "My other teachers can help balance your version with our recorded history, giving the children a better idea of the full truth. But I want to start the next generation on thinking that they can change the status quo instead of just putting up with it."

Bram was cleverer than she'd originally given him credit for. "As long as there's a dragon-shifter adult there too, in case things go wrong, I'll try."

Bram smiled. "Good. You'll start in three days."

Mel didn't like the devious look in Bram's eye, but at least she wouldn't have to spend all of her time here doing nothing. Children were usually more honest and more open than adults were. She could probably learn just as much from them as they would from her.

Her only reservation was that Tristan taught the young dragon-shifters. If Bram thought to play matchmaker, he wasn't going to be successful. Unless Tristan groveled and pleaded, which was highly unlikely, she wasn't going to put herself out there only to have him shoot her down again.

The dragonman had made his choice. No matter how much she missed his presence in bed next to her, she wasn't going to put up with his bullshit just so she could feel his hot, naked skin against hers again. The heartache wasn't worth it.

CHAPTER NINE

Melanie stood in front of four pupils in the five-to-six-year-old age range. The dragon-shifter teacher was introducing her, but Melanie didn't pay much attention to what the dragonwoman was saying. Instead, she focused everything on remaining calm on the outside and not betraying the butterflies banging around in her stomach.

Don't let the little ones smell fear, or they'll walk all over you. That had been Liam's advice to her before she'd left this morning. People who taught human students probably gave the same advice, but since she'd been told how the five-and-six-year-olds were just learning to communicate with their inner dragons, not showing fear was doubly important—the newly awakened dragons were trying to find their own place in the dominance scale.

However, the longer she studied the faces of the three little boys and one little girl, the more confident she became. They weren't staring at her with disgust or condemnation. No, they were just staring at her with wide-eyed curiosity.

The teacher turned toward her and nodded. Melanie nodded back and focused on the four students. "As the teacher said, my name is Melanie Hall. And I think the best way to get to know each other is for you to just ask your burning questions now."

The little girl with dark hair and blue eyes raised her hand, and Melanie motioned for the girl to speak.

The little girl looked her up and down before she said, "My friend said humans aren't allowed on Stonefire's land because they'll either scream or try to hurt us. Are you going to scream or hurt us?"

"No, I'm not. Should I be afraid of you?"

The little girl crossed her arms over her chest and it took everything Mel had not to smile. The girl said, "Well, I know important people. So you should be good or I can tell on you and my uncle will make you behave. He makes everyone behave."

The teacher said, "Ava." But Mel put up a hand to signal it was okay. "So, your name is Ava?" The little girl nodded. "Well, Ava, is your uncle here right now?"

The girl's arms dropped as she lost a bit of her confidence. "No."

She took a step toward the girl. "Could he get here before I could tackle you?"

Ava darted a glance to the dragon-shifter teacher and back. "No."

Mel stood right in front of the little girl and placed a hand on her head. "Then using him as a threat is useless. You should always be thinking of how to take care of yourself in the moment."

The little girl stared up at her with awe. After another second, Mel crouched down and tickled the girl's sides. Ava started giggling and squirming, and Mel stopped but remained crouched to look Ava in the eye. "What do you think? Do you reckon I'm going to run off screaming or try to hurt you?"

Ava stared at her for a second before she answered, "I don't think so."

"Why not?"

"Because Drustan only tickles me because he fancies me. Do you fancy me, Ms. Hall?"

Mel laughed. "Not in that way, Ava. But I think I like you."

Ava beamed and Mel stood up to talk with the other children. Within a few minutes, they were all relaxed and chattering away in the way young children did. She'd never thought of herself as a teacher, but maybe this teaching thing wouldn't be so bad after all.

~~~

Tristan stood inside Melanie's empty cottage and tried his best to forget what he'd done here less than six days ago. Spending time with the young had indeed calmed his beast to a level Tristan could control. But right now, upon finding Melanie was no longer staying here, his dragon was snarling for him to find her. Now.

Her scent was nearly gone. Only through sheer force of will did he resist finding something that still carried her scent so he could bring it up to his nose and brand her smell into his memory.

Of course, that was his dragon's need hammering inside his head. It'd taken him five days to calm the bastard down, yet at the first whiff of the human, his hard work had all but evaporated.

Fucking fantastic.

He turned and left the cottage. If he was going to investigate the human, he needed to find her first. She could only be in one of two places. He decided to start with Bram since Samira would probably bar him outright from talking with her.

SACRIFICED TO THE DRAGON

That human female could be as fierce and protective as any dragonwoman.

After knocking on Bram's door, Tristan entered to find a nervous Cait on the far side of the room, her eyes downcast. Since he knew how easily she spooked, he remained silent and kept his distance. Bram flashed him a look of thanks and then said to the woman, "That's all for now, Cait. You can go."

The woman nodded, and rushed out the back entrance. Once the door clicked closed, Bram turned toward him, and Tristan said, "Since when does Caitriona Belmont leave her cottage alone?"

"Since Melanie Hall started visiting her."

What has she been doing? Where is she now? I want her. Why can't I have her?

He silenced his inner dragon and said, "Where is Melanie now?"

Bram sat down in his chair behind his desk. "It's taken you five days to ask me that question, which means either you truly do hate her, or you're fighting yourself because of what happened to your mother."

He growled. "You seem bloody trusting with the human female considering how little we know about her."

"Ah, but you see, you're wrong about that. She's won over my niece. And if Melanie Hall can win over Ava, I'm confident she can win over most of the clan in time. Her straightforward-yet-kind manner has already won over Cait, Samira, Liam, Liam's siblings, and three of your fellow teachers. The one who's judging her without knowing her is you, Tristan MacLeod. But that's about to change."

The mention of some of the other teachers made him suspicious. "Not that it's any of your fucking business, but how?"

Bram raised an eyebrow. "We've been friends nearly our whole lives, but even if that wasn't enough to care about your stubborn arse, the way you treat the mother of one of our clan is most definitely my business." He grunted, knowing Bram was right, and his clan leader continued, "Melanie has been working with the young dragons, and from tomorrow, she's going to spend three mornings a week with your pupils."

Three entire mornings in Melanie's presence a week would most definitely set off his dragon. While he personally was trying not to think what it'd be like to fuck her sweet, tight pussy again, he was going to hide behind the excuse of his students' safety. "And if my dragon gains control, what then? The scent of my child will trigger the beast's instincts."

Bram shrugged. "If you were living with her and fucking her on a regular basis, it wouldn't be a problem. But since you're letting your prejudice get in the way of recognizing how wonderful the human female is, then you have to deal with those consequences. If it means resigning from your teaching job because you can't get your shit together, so be it."

"Bram—"

"No. This discussion is over. As clan leader, I'm kicking your arse out of my office so I can do some work."

Tristan clenched his jaw. Pulling his clan leader title out had been enough to stop him from arguing, as Bram well knew. "Fine. Will you at least tell me if she's staying with Samira?"

"Yes. Now get the hell out and go deal with your bloody issues. They're giving me a headache."

Tristan turned on his heel before he said something he'd regret and left.

He had planned to visit Melanie, but now that he knew he would have to spend tomorrow morning with her, he needed to retreat to the teaching area. If he didn't calm his dragon down again, his beast wouldn't care if children were present or not, it'd jump the female at the first whiff of her scent.

~ ~ ~

Melanie made her way to today's training area. It was her third day of working with the students, and she'd discovered that without all of the bias and hatred of the adults, she loved interacting with the young dragon-shifters. They were as curious about her as she was about them, which would be a welcome distraction in the coming months. Especially since she'd been told that human women who were pregnant with a dragon-shifter child usually developed morning sickness faster than if she were having a human baby. As it was, the smells of certain foods were already making her queasy.

She placed a hand over her belly and smiled. After winning over Ava Moore-Llewellyn, whom she'd later learned was Bram's niece, Melanie actually looked forward to being a mother. Even if her baby was stubborn when he or she got older, all of this time teaching had taught her how to not only handle difficult children, but also what to expect when it came time to deal with her child's emerging dragon. Apparently, since the shifting gene was dominant, all human females who had a dragon-shifter's baby would have a little child capable of one day shifting, too.

That was something else she wished she'd found out during her research before coming here. Not that it mattered; she was determined to stay and raise her child. But it might help with other women who were on the fence about whether to sacrifice themselves or not.

She just hoped her child would take after her and not Tristan. The asshole had yet to say anything to her since he'd scented her pregnancy a week ago.

Don't think about him. She had friends, a purpose, and an entire culture to study. If she could contact her family or let them visit, it would almost be perfect.

Of course, she had weeks before she'd be granted communication privileges, and only then if Tristan said so. Maybe if she excelled at this teaching thing, then Bram would grant her the privileges regardless.

Mel came up to the rock ridge sheltering the practice areas used for the young dragon-shifters. Since it was early summer, the teachers tried to bring the students outside as much as the northern English weather allowed, using the few months of sunshine for shifting practice.

She had yet to see any of the children attempt to shift, but hopefully the longer she worked with the teachers, the more they'd open up to her and let her watch some of their lessons. After all, she was a child when it came to dragon-shifter ways and if she was going to spend the rest of her life here, she needed to start catching up.

She came to the ten-foot-wide gap between the rock walls that formed an entrance to one of the "safe areas" used for the youngest children and stopped to wait for a natural break in the lesson to approach the teacher. But as she looked over at the far side of the clearing, she barely noticed the ten students. No, her eyes latched on to the tall figure of Tristan MacLeod.

He was currently talking to his students. She couldn't hear what he was saying, but the frown and broody attitude was mostly gone. Instead, Tristan had a patient, yet firm look on his face as he motioned for one of the students to come up front.

94

SACRIFICED TO THE DRAGON

The little boy moved to stand next to Tristan. After listening to his teacher, the little boy closed his eyes. A few seconds later, his hand became something that wasn't a hand—she was too far away to see clearly, but she guessed it was a dragon claw—and then opened his eyes to shout, "I did it!"

The sound echoed down to her, and she smiled as Tristan gave the boy's shoulder a squeeze. After saying something else, the boy's hand returned to a pale human one. The other students cheered as the boy went to stand back with his classmates.

Tristan was even smiling as he watched the boy return to his place. Then Tristan's eyes roamed over his students, as if he were trying to think of whom to pick next, when his gaze found hers.

Even from this distance, his look sent a little thrill through her body. Melanie remembered everything he—and by extension, she—had done less than a week ago. Such as the feel of his hands on her ass; the sting of his bite on her neck; the fullness of his cock inside her as he took her against a wall.

The growl he made when he came.

Her cheeks went hot, but she didn't break his gaze. She wasn't embarrassed about their marathon of fantastic sex, let alone afraid of him, and she wanted to make sure he knew it.

With a deep inhalation and exhalation, she squared her shoulders, pasted a patient smile on her face, and strode toward the end of the clearing. By now, the students all turned to see what their teacher was staring at. When she was close enough, she could hear their murmurs of "Who is she?", "Do we have a guest?", and finally, when she was less than ten feet from them, "Why does she smell like Mr. MacLeod?"

Before either she or Tristan could say anything, one of the little girls said, "I know why! She smells like him because she's carrying Mr. MacLeod's baby! My mama smelled like my dad before my brother was born."

The other students started to chatter, but then Tristan said, "Quiet," and the students stopped talking.

She moved to stand next to Tristan. Despite the frown on his face, she remembered the patient version of him with the student, and she yearned to have that version of him holding her against his warm chest. That man she could actually like.

But the guarded look he always seemed to carry when she was around was back. It was best to get on with why she was here.

She raised an eyebrow and said, "They must've told you I would come to teach. Aren't you going to introduce me to your students?"

CHAPTER TEN

From the instant Tristan had met Melanie's gaze, he'd had to battle both his attraction to her and the demands of his dragon.

With the children standing in front of him, his dragon was behaving—for the moment. The beast only thought of fucking her once every thirty seconds, which was only marginally better than having a constant need and desire broadcast inside his head.

When she stood next to him, the mixture of her feminine scent with his, because of the pregnancy, caused an overwhelming protectiveness to rush through his body.

Why did you abandon her? She is ours. We should take her home. Treasure her. Pleasure her. Fuck her.

Not right now. I need to help the young. Or do you want to leave them vulnerable? That thought silenced his dragon. Protecting the young was the most important.

Melanie asked if he was going to introduce her, and he turned to his morning class. "This is Miss Melanie Hall. You've probably scented it already, but she is a human female. From today, she's going to come at least once a week to teach you human studies." He turned toward Melanie. "They're all yours."

He barely registered what she said next as he studied the curve of her cheek, or the way the sun cast red glints in her hair. Her top clung to her breasts as if to tempt him, much like her jeans hugged her nice, wide hips and soft arse, reminding him what it was like to fuck her from behind.

Everything about her body called to him.

He resisted a frown. What the bloody hell was wrong with him? He'd never felt such attraction to a woman before. Determined not to fall prey to her luscious, curvy body, he turned his gaze back to his students. He just caught Melanie telling them to ask her anything, and Misa's hand shot up.

Mel nodded and the little girl said, "So, was I right? Are you carrying Mr. MacLeod's baby?"

He watched Melanie cross her arms over her chest. Only through an ironclad will did he avoid looking at them as she said, "Yes. But since dragon-shifters also get pregnant and have babies, how about asking me something related to human ways?"

One of the boys shouted, "I heard that humans like to collect dragon teeth and talons and wear them around their necks. Is that true?"

"Hundreds of years ago, yes, it was. However, since then, things have changed. These days, there is a type of truce between most humans and dragon-shifters."

The boy looked unconvinced. "Then why do some humans hunt us?"

Tristan was keen to hear her answer. Melanie took a second, and then said, "Because just like with dragon-shifters, some humans will always be jerks and will ignore the rules."

"Are you one of the jerks?"

Melanie smiled. "No, I don't think so. I've actually studied dragon-shifters for years. Someday, I want to write a book and help get rid of the nasty rumors."

That piqued Tristan's curiosity. Was the female being sincere or just saying what the children wanted to hear?

One of the other boys said, "Which rumors? Like, do all humans think we're strong and fierce monsters? Or I've also heard they think we steal their belongings in the middle of the night. And there's the one about us breathing fire. Or..."

As the boy rattled off all the old stories and rumors about their kind, Tristan watched as Melanie calmly answered and dispelled most of them. Considering how tight-lipped the dragons were, she knew an astounding amount about them. He wasn't sure if that made him more or less suspicious of her.

By the time the lunch cart was being rolled toward the students, it was clear that she'd won over his pupils by being honest and open. She never dismissed them as too young to understand or said their questions were silly or daft.

Tristan started to wonder if Bram's words were true and that his mistrust of her was unfounded.

But he would talk with her in private before making any final decisions on what to do with her.

He raised a hand in greeting at the middle-aged dragonwoman rolling the lunch cart toward them. The scent of warm roast beef hit his nose and his stomach growled. While dragon-shifters weren't carnivores, their beasts always loved the smell and taste of meat.

He turned to dismiss the students for lunch when he saw Melanie holding a hand to her mouth and looking rather pale. He glanced around, but he didn't see any threats. He moved to her side. "What's wrong? Are you ill?"

She nodded and dashed for the far side of the clearing, leaned over, and dry heaved. He asked the lunch attendant to keep an eye on his students and he went to Melanie's side. Without thinking, he rubbed her back as she lost what must've been her breakfast.

~~~

As soon as the smell of roasted meat had hit her nose, Mel's stomach had started churning right before the nausea hit her. Apparently, her early morning sickness had decided to rear its ugly head in front of Tristan of all people.

To avoid embarrassing herself by getting sick all over him, she rushed away from Tristan and the children to a spot near the wall of rock. She dry-heaved for about thirty seconds before her breakfast finally came up, burning her throat. At some point, a warm hand caressed her back, and the reassuring, warm touch made her feel a little better.

When she had nothing left to vomit, she stood up and a blue reusable water bottle was thrust in front of her face. Tristan said, "Here. Take it."

Wanting to get rid of the awful taste in her mouth, she took it without a word, rinsed out her mouth, and spit out the water. After a few sips of water, she started to feel somewhat normal again.

And to think, she had months of this to look forward to. At least she had Samira and Liam to help her through the worst of it.

After one more deep breath, she looked up to thank Tristan for the water, but her words died in her throat at the fierce look in his eyes. The look kicked her temper into gear, and before she could stop herself, she said, "What have I done now to deserve that look? Is my vomit, caused by your baby by the way, offending your sensitive dragon nose?"

He growled. "No. You're ill and my dragon doesn't like it."

She'd been civil in front of the children, but she decided to let loose in a quiet, steely voice. "Oh, that's right. Only your dragon cares about me because I'm breeding. You are perfectly all right to ditch me at the first scent of pregnancy." She waved toward the students. "Go eat your lunch, Tristan. My time is up, so I'll leave you alone for today."

She moved to leave when Tristan's hands clamped around her upper arms. "I will see you home."

She gave a pointed look at the grip on her arm and back to his face. "Why? I can walk, and you made it clear that I'm on my own. I fulfilled my end of the sacrifice contract by conceiving and I don't need your protection. If something happens, Samira or Liam will help me."

As soon as she mentioned Liam's name, Tristan's pupils flashed to slits and back again. "You shouldn't be asking another male to look after you."

Aware of the children, Melanie kept her anger to a restrained whisper. "You gave up any claim as to what I do or who I ask for help the instant you snuck out and left me alone in that bed."

"I have my reasons for doing that, but you wouldn't understand."

She narrowed her eyes. "If this is about what happened to your mother and sister, I know about that."

His fierce look grew fiercer. "Who told you?"

"All that matters is that I know. And while focusing hatred on all humans might seem like a fine idea to you, it's useless, Tristan. And I would think you'd see that if you only gave me a chance."

"Giving you a chance would mean being near you. As long as I remain with the children, my beast's need to claim you is replaced by a need to protect the young. If I meet with you anywhere else, even in front of others, my dragon will push to the forefront and seek you out." He leaned down until his breath was hot on her ear and whispered, "My inner beast is already attached to you. I guarantee that if you let me fuck you even just one more time, I won't be able to keep my dragon away from you as I've been doing the past week. And you remember what happened the last time my dragon broke loose, and that's just a glimpse of what could happen."

~~~

He was trying to scare her away from him. For himself, or because of his dragon's throbbing need to claim her, he didn't know. As he waited for her reply, he was overly aware of her womanly scent filling his nose, making him hard all over again. He was tempted to lick her ear, but he had just enough self-control to stop himself.

Take her home. Care for her. Protect her. Let the other dragon watch the children.

His dragon was starting to demand more than just sex; the beast wanted to look after her.

Fuck, that wasn't good. The attachment was getting stronger, and after the last half-hour of watching Melanie deal with the children before being sick, even the human-half of him was starting to wonder if he'd been too harsh on her.

Melanie turned her head to look him in the eye. "Before I let you fuck me again, Tristan, I want to meet your sister."

His dragon hummed. *She wants to fuck us. I want her. We must do anything to make her ours. Then next time, she won't want to leave us.*

Tristan gritted his teeth, ignored his dragon, and focused on Melanie's request as he said, "My sister likes humans even less than I do."

"You're really going for the gold with your compliments, aren't you?"

He growled, his arousal dimmed by anger. "This isn't a laughing matter. They beat my sister within an inch of her life, and if my mother hadn't succeeded in distracting the human dragon hunters, my sister would've been raped and butchered for parts just like what had happened with my mother."

Melanie's look softened. "Tristan, I'm so sorry."

"I didn't ask for your pity."

"It's not pity. I'm being sincere, as I couldn't imagine what that would be like." She put a hand on his chest and the touch soothed his anger a fraction. "But believe me, I'm not an undercover dragon hunter. I'm going to be the mother of your child. Doesn't that count for something?"

He stared at her for a second and decided he needed to ask her something before he brought her anywhere near his sister.

He resisted a frown. Why was he thinking of introducing her to his sister? Meeting with a human was the last thing Arabella needed.

But the curiosity that had been bouncing around inside his head was strong enough to make him ask his question anyway. "Did you mean what you said earlier to the students, about wanting to write a book to help stop the nasty rumors about us?"

Mel nodded. "Yes. At first, I just wanted to find something unique for my doctoral thesis, but after three days of teaching the children of this clan, I want to help build a better future for them. The bias and discrimination will never completely disappear, but it'd be nice if humans and dragon-shifters could interact without living in perpetual fear of trying to kill each other."

There was no trace of deceit or fear in her scent. That told him the human believed in her words.

Had Bram been right to say he was letting his prejudice get in the way? Even if it was true, and he wasn't entirely convinced it was, he still had his sister to think about. Arabella was his only family, and if she couldn't get past Melanie being human, there was no way he could have both Melanie and his sister in his life if Melanie decided to stay after their child was born.

As if sensing his doubts, Melanie added, "Believe me, I know what it's like to want to protect your family." She gave a faint smile. "After all, I came here to save my brother's life."

She stared down at her hand on his chest. As she started to stroke him, some of the tension eased out of his body. Her voice was soft when she continued, "I swear on my brother Oliver's life that I'm not trying to deceive you or do anything to intentionally hurt your sister." She looked back into his eyes. "And if that's not enough, I'll swear it on the life of our unborn child. Please, Tristan, let me meet your sister and see if I can help her get past her fear of humans."

"Why do you seem so intent on helping everyone? First Cait, now offering for my sister. What's in it for you?"

"I could ask the same thing, about you teaching the young dragon-shifters. It's just something I do without thinking. I can't stand to see people hurting who have a chance at happiness."

Believe her, his dragon crooned.

A small part of him hidden deep, deep inside agreed with the beast. But the human-half asked, "Is that what I am to you? A fix-it project?"

She frowned. "I just want to get to know the father of my baby. Is that too much to ask?"

He was suspicious of Melanie's ulterior motives. But with his dragon urging him to agree and the deeply buried part of him which remembered being interested in humans as a boy coming back to the forefront of his mind, Tristan decided to give Melanie a chance. Just one. If she betrayed it, he'd find a way to stay away from her, even if it meant leaving the clan for a few months.

Decision made, he said, "Wait here for a second. I'll be right back."

She blinked at his order, but nodded. He reluctantly released his grip on her arms and went to the dragonwoman currently handing out student lunches. Each step he took away from the human made his inner beast try to crawl out and take control. Tristan said, *Let me take care of the young and then I will go back to her.*

I don't believe you.

I'm telling the truth, so let me do what needs to be done. Otherwise, she will leave without us. Is that what you want?

His inner beast growled. *No. Hurry up.*

Once his dragon retreated, Tristan approached the dragonwoman handing out lunches. As soon as he was close enough, he said, "Can you watch the children and take them to their next class? I need to take care of the mother of my child."

The dragonwoman darted a glance toward Melanie, but instead of the disdain he'd expected, the older woman had sympathy in her eyes. The dragonwoman nodded. "I remember what it's like to get morning sickness, and it's ten times worse for humans carrying one of our children. Take her home and pamper her, Tristan. Humans are so fragile, and who knows if these next nine months will be her last."

No, she will NOT die, his dragon screamed inside his head.

He pushed the beast back and said to the female, "So you don't care that she's an outsider on our land?"

The woman, Lia, if he remembered right, shook her head. "Why would I? She's helping our clan's future by coming here and being willing to bear one of our children, despite the risks to her life and her reputation if she leaves here after the child is born."

"You're in the minority, then."

Lia shrugged. "Maybe. But all that matters is that you take care of her, Tristan. I've heard the rumors about you not even checking in on her this past week, and it's disappointing. I knew your mum, and no matter what race the mother of her grandchild was, she would've expected you to take care of your future family."

He made a noncommittal noise. He wasn't about to discuss his mother with who knew how many students listening to his conversation. What Lia had already said was bad enough. He turned and said, "I'm going now."

Without looking back, he walked over to Melanie. As he approached her, he caught the human's scent and his dragon growled. Only when he put a hand on Melanie's lower back did the beast fall quiet again. No doubt, it was semi-behaving because Melanie had just been sick.

Funny, that. His dragon stopped thinking about fucking her whenever she threw up. Morning sickness might work to his advantage.

He pushed against her back. "Come with me."

Melanie looked up at him. "Where are we going?"

Without thinking, his hand started to rub her lower back. "You're going to get cleaned up and then we're going to pay a visit to my sister, Arabella."

CHAPTER ELEVEN

As Tristan led Melanie toward Samira and Liam's cottage to freshen up before visiting his sister, Lia's words from back at the clearing kept ringing inside his head: *I knew your mum, and no matter what race the mother of her grandchild was, she would've expected you to take care of your future family.*

He didn't want to admit it, but Lia was right. Due to the brutal, tragic nature of his mother's death, he rarely remembered what she'd been like when she had been alive. Part of the reason he'd been interested in humans as a boy had been because of his mother. Jocelyn MacLeod had believed much as Bram did today, in that she'd envisioned a future where dragon-shifters and humans would work together.

From what little information he'd extracted from his sister, their mum had believed that up until the end.

After Melanie's interactions with the children, and Bram's support, he was pretty confident that Melanie wasn't working with the dragon hunters. But the real test would be if she could win over his sister or not. Arabella had gone through things that would make a lesser person give up on life. While she mostly kept to herself because of her lack of trust in others, she had found a way to help the clan by studying computer programming.

However, his sister was quite antisocial, to the point she may not open the door to let Melanie inside her home. He'd just have to make sure his sister could scent that Melanie was carrying his child. The faint trace of his scent in the human's skin might be enough to convince Arabella to give her a chance, instead of slamming the door in their faces and retreating back to in front of her computer.

And for reasons he couldn't explain, he wanted Arabella to open the door and give Melanie a chance.

As they passed one of the Stonefire's eateries, the smell of steak and kidney pie filled his nose, making his stomach rumble. No doubt, after losing her breakfast, Melanie would be hungry too.

He was about to ask her if she wanted something to eat when she buried her head against his chest and wrapped her arms around his waist. He stopped walking and said, "What's wrong?"

Her voice was muffled. "That smell...it makes me want to vomit again."

"So you're burying your face against me to cover me in sick and get revenge on me for impregnating you?"

She shook her head against his chest. "For some reason, your scent calms my stomach."

His inner dragon hummed. *Our scent helps her. She will want us always by her side.*

Tristan brushed the remark aside, determined to remain unaffected. "Let's keep going. We're nearly there."

"If I move my head away before we clear that smell, I'll be sick. And this time, I'll make sure to aim for you."

He nearly smiled. Even when facing a humiliating situation, like being sick in public, Melanie Hall didn't back down.

Since she was suffering in part because of him, he looped an arm around her waist and said, "I can carry you or guide you until the smell clears. Which method do you prefer?"

She hesitated a second and then said, "Guide me, but make sure to walk slowly."

His dragon let out a soft snarl inside his head. *Carry her. I want to feel her soft body pressed against ours.*

Not now. She doesn't feel well. Comfort her first and maybe we'll feel her body against ours later. At the promise of feeling the human female's curves against his skin, the dragon retreated. Tristan tried not to think too hard on how cooperative his beast was being, because that would mean thinking about how attached his dragon was becoming to the human.

He tightened his grip on Melanie's waist and started walking, careful to time his steps to her sideways walk. He nearly ordered her to walk faster, but then he remembered Lia's words about taking care of Melanie. If his mother were alive today and saw him barking at a pregnant woman, carrying his baby no less, she would've frowned and give him a cool, even look. His mother had never been one to raise her voice, yet Tristan and his sister had known better than to disobey her.

Thinking about his mother squeezed his heart. He'd pretty much locked away his memories of her for both his and Arabella's sakes, but he was starting to wonder if it was time to address both the pain and the memories of his mum. He had a feeling that during their visit with Arabella, he wouldn't have a choice.

Samira and Liam's cottage came into view and he caught traces of Liam's scent in the air. His dragon snarled and tried to take control. *A male lives inside that house. He will take our human many times until he erases our scent. We must take her away and protect her from all other males.*

I will protect her. Now, stop being daft. Liam has his own mate.

But ours is better.

Ignoring the remark about mates, Tristan said, *Stop it or I will shut you out completely.*

His dragon grumbled and allowed Tristan's human-half to remain in control. At least, for the time being.

He tightened his grip on the human to further soothe his dragon. The feel of her soft curves warm against his hand, arm, and chest calmed the beast. He hoped Liam was out, or his dragon would try everything he could to break free, resulting in a rather spectacular display of protectiveness and possibly a fight.

They reached the front door of Samira's cottage. Tristan gave his dragon one last warning to behave before he said, "We're here."

~ ~ ~

Melanie had mixed feelings about morning sickness. On the one hand, ordinary smells made her want to vomit on a second's notice. On the other hand, it made Tristan be nice to her.

It was strange having her face pressed against his chest as he guided her toward Samira's cottage, but she hadn't lied about his scent calming her stomach. She didn't know if it had to do with the half-dragon baby in her uterus or not, but whatever the reason, it beat throwing up again.

Yet as they slowly moved toward Liam and Samira's cottage, she couldn't help but notice the heat of his hand on her waist or how safe she felt pressed up against him. If he continued being nice to her, she probably would jump into bed with him again at the first opportunity. And if that happened, she had no idea what Tristan's inner dragon would do. She wasn't quite sure what it meant for one to "grow attached" as he'd put it. For all she knew, it might curb her freedom on Stonefire's land rather than expand it.

Not that she'd allow him the opportunity to try to contain her. She'd worked hard for what freedoms she'd gained thus far, and she'd fight for them all over again if she had to.

Still, despite all of that, she couldn't help but wonder if an attached dragon looked something like how Liam and Samira acted with one another. Strong-willed Samira melted whenever Liam caressed her cheek or gave her a gentle kiss. While staying with the pair, she'd never seen Liam try to hide his affection.

Sometimes Liam's possessiveness surfaced when another adult male was in the room and he'd haul Samira up against his side, but Samira never seemed to mind. Quite the opposite, actually; she'd lean against him and lay her head on his shoulder.

Stop it, Hall. No fairy tale endings, remember? Melanie resisted a sigh, realizing she was hoping for things she probably would never have. Tristan wasn't Liam. Hell, if not for Tristan's dragon, the man would probably have nothing to do with her.

And that stung a little.

Before she could think too hard about why it did, Tristan said, "We're here."

She eased her head up and looked at Tristan towering over her. "Did the smell last the entire way here?"

He shrugged, but didn't comment. She hoped this wasn't a sign of Tristan-the-asshole returning.

Since she lived with Samira now, she took out her key from her pocket and unlocked the door. Unsure if anyone was home, she opened the door and was instantly attacked by a little boy flying at her as he said, "Auntie Mel!"

The boy hugged her legs as she put her hand on the head of Samira's three-year-old son, Rhys. Smiling, Melanie said, "Someone should be about due for a nap."

Rhys looked up at her, a small frown between his black eyebrows. "No, it's not nap time. It's lunch time."

That would explain the smell of curry spices in the air. Thankfully, it didn't make her stomach turn. "Where's your mom and dad?"

"Dad's gone. Mum's in the kitchen." Rhys looked around Mel's legs and said, "Who's he?"

She turned and waved toward Tristan. "This is Tristan MacLeod. In a few years, he might be your teacher. So if I were you, I'd be nice to him."

Rhys assessed Tristan with an over-the-top seriousness and Melanie barely resisted laughing. Finally, the boy said, "My mum doesn't like you."

She glanced at Tristan and bit her lip to keep from laughing at the momentary surprise on his face. But just as quickly as it had arrived, it was replaced with a cool, collected one. Tristan raised an eyebrow and said, "Care to tell me why?"

The boy squeezed her legs tightly and said, "Because you're mean to Auntie Mel."

The little boy's protectiveness went straight to her heart. It seemed that trait manifested early in dragon-shifter males.

Now was not the time for a conversation about how Tristan should treat her. If everything went well with his sister, she'd be initiating that conversation herself.

To change the subject, she pried Rhys from her legs and maneuvered him toward the kitchen. "Let's go see your mom about lunch. Whatever she made smells good."

SACRIFICED TO THE DRAGON

The boy reluctantly nodded and let her lead him into the kitchen in the back of the two-story cottage.

They entered the warm kitchen filled with smells that made her mouth water, which was a nice change from earlier. Samira smiled when she saw them, but her smile instantly faded as soon as she spotted Tristan behind her.

~~~

Tristan watched Melanie lead the little boy out of the room and while she hadn't invited him to follow, he did anyway.

The sight of Liam and Samira's son had put his dragon in the background, which was a good thing considering his beast didn't like Melanie staying in another male's house. Even now, he could smell the other male, and neither half of him liked it.

Liam was a nice enough bloke, but even though Liam was mated to Samira, Tristan's dragon was in a dangerous in-between stage when it came to Melanie. Seeing any adult male put a hand on Melanie could set off his inner beast and his human-half could lose control.

As he entered the kitchen, Samira didn't see him at first and she greeted Melanie with a smile, but it died when she looked at him. "What's he doing here?" She glanced to Melanie. "Did he grovel and beg for you to take him back?"

He should hold his tongue, but he'd never been very good at that when it came to conversing with adults. "It's none of your business, Samira. What is between Melanie and me is our business."

Samira held up the wooden spoon in her hand and pointed it at him. "Seeing as your bastard ways have made it so she's staying with me, it's very much my business. I was on your side originally, Tristan MacLeod, but not anymore."

Before he could reply, Melanie stepped between them. "Stop it." She looked to Samira. "I'm just here to change my clothes and brush my teeth. Can I leave you guys alone for a few minutes while I do that and not worry about you two biting off each other's heads?"

Samira lowered her spoon and stirred the contents of a pot on the stove in front of her. "Don't you both have classes to teach this afternoon?"

Tristan beat Melanie to the reply. "Not anymore. Melanie's morning sickness hit, and while she's changing, I'm going to let Bram know and ask someone to cover for us."

Samira's expression softened as she looked at Melanie again. "Are you feeling okay now?"

Melanie nodded. "I'll be fine." She shot Tristan a look. "And I have something to do before Tristan changes his mind."

Samira looked between them, but Melanie didn't elaborate. Good. The human female was siding with him about keeping their business to themselves.

His dragon had been following the exchange, afraid someone might upset his human female, and now, it urged Tristan to give their female some kind of assurance. *The other male is gone for now. She isn't in danger. We should soothe her worries. Tell her we won't cause any trouble.*

Rather than fight his inner beast, Tristan said, "I won't start anything. Go change."

Melanie looked unconvinced, but she finally nodded and went upstairs. When she was gone, Samira asked, "Where are you taking her?"

114

Tristan shook his head. "I'm not telling you." He pulled out his mobile phone from his pocket. "Now excuse me, I need to ring Bram before Melanie comes back downstairs."

He turned to go into the living room but found the little boy standing in his way. Tristan raised an eyebrow, but the little boy just crossed his arms over his chest and stood his ground. This little one was going to be quite the handful when his dragon finally started communicating with him in a few years' time.

Still, Tristan had spent more than a decade teaching children and he'd found being straightforward with them was usually the best policy. "Is there something you want to say to me, little one?" The boy nodded and Tristan said, "Well, go on then."

"Be nice to Auntie Mel and don't make her cry."

Tristan's dragon growled at the thought of Melanie crying.

Rather than argue with the child, he gave him a direct stare and said, "I need to get through. If you have anything else to say, then say it."

The boy's confidence faltered under the gaze of his. "That's it."

Tristan nodded. "Right. Then let me pass."

The little boy moved aside and Tristan went to the far end of the living room where he'd be safe from Samira's human hearing. He didn't want anyone to know about his asking for this afternoon and tomorrow off. If things went well with his sister, they would stay the night at her cottage. If not, then Tristan needed a few private hours with Melanie to lay out the future when it came to their child and divided responsibilities.

He already knew which outcome his dragon was rooting for, but the human-half was unsure. To be honest, both halves of him were starting to hope Melanie would be able to help his sister. To wish for anything else would be selfish and unkind.

Of course, there was also the caveat that if Melanie helped Arabella, the human might let him fuck her on a regular basis, allowing him to better control his dragon.

But that was all to come. Right now, he dialed Bram's phone number and tried not to think about how complicated things might become if his dragon-half became fully attached. When that happened, he would be forced to start courting Melanie or risk being completely lost to his beast.

On top of that, the little boy's accusation of him making Melanie cry didn't sit well, and if nothing else, he would make sure she didn't cry again because of his actions. He didn't want to become like Neil. The idea of Melanie becoming a broken recluse like Caitriona Belmont caused his dragon to growl as well as leave a sour taste in his mouth.

No, with a little effort, he could be civil. He couldn't promise her anything else, but he could at least prevent her from being completely miserable because of his bastard ways.

Chapter Twelve

With a fresh change of clothes and clean teeth, Melanie felt almost normal again. The piece of warm naan bread she'd swiped from Samira's kitchen on her way out had simultaneously calmed her stomach and stopped it from rumbling. A good thing, too, since their destination was turning out to be quite a hike from the main Stonefire living area.

While Mel had had some time to explore the "city center" equivalent of Stonefire's community, they were heading somewhere new, away from the nearby lake and toward one of the hills not quite tall enough to be called a mountain. The contrast of the flat land with the sharp, jagged hills and mountains was breathtaking. She could see why people liked to holiday in the human sections of the Lake District.

She and Tristan had walked mostly in awkward silence, but when a lone cottage came into view, she asked, "Is that where your sister lives?"

"Yes. Arabella likes her peace and quiet."

Mel had a feeling there was a deeper issue keeping Arabella away from everyone else, but she merely nodded. The last thing she wanted was to start an argument with Tristan. If his sister was anything like Cait, then she wouldn't like strangers or unannounced visits. An argument could easily upset her or make her close in on herself, which reminded her, "Did you tell her we were coming?"

"No. If it were just me, Ara would stay put. But if she knew you were coming, she'd hike around the surrounding countryside for the rest of the afternoon."

"Because she doesn't like visitors or because I'm human?"

"Both."

Mel knew she should keep her mouth shut, but she couldn't do it. "I hope you're starting to realize not all humans are bad, Tristan. Because if not, I should just leave right now."

He glanced over at her. "So if I said I still hated all humans, you'd leave?"

She didn't want to answer him, but she needed to stand her ground with the dragonman. "Yes."

He grabbed her wrist and pulled her to a stop. "Before I give you my verdict, I want to know why you care so much for my opinion. You said yourself that you fulfilled your end of the contract, as have I. There is no reason for us to pretend for the sake of the child. I've heard that you want to stay afterward, but if family is so important to you, would you be able to live the rest of your life here without them? Humans aren't allowed on Stonefire's land, Melanie, unless they either come as a sacrifice or are with the UK Department of Dragon Affairs."

She narrowed her eyes. "I do love my family, but I'm a grown woman, Tristan, and I'm not about to leave my child behind, no matter how much I'm starting to think you'd do a good job of raising him or her."

His grip eased a fraction. "You barely know me. Why would you say that?"

"I watched you with the children before you noticed me. With no one watching, you were kind, patient, and understanding.

Whatever your issue with humans, I believe what I saw back in the clearing is your true self. You may never act that way around me, and that's fine. But I can easily see you acting that way with our child, and that's the kind of father I'd want for my baby."

~ ~ ~

Tristan had remained silent on the walk to his sister's place to avoid saying something he'd regret. He couldn't promise anything until he knew how things played out with Arabella.

But when Melanie pushed him on the issue of humans, he hadn't been able to hold back. The last thing he'd expected to hear from her lips was that he'd make a good father.

He wanted to say he bloody well would be a good father; no one would ever harm his child. But talking of their child meant talking about the future. Tristan never made a promise he couldn't keep, and all too easily, he could see himself starting to make tentative plans with the human. She intrigued both the man and the beast with her ability to stand up to him, face a new culture and a new way of doing things, all without blinking an eye.

But no matter what he was starting to think of Melanie Hall, he would never do anything to harm his sister. The sooner he introduced her to Arabella, the sooner he could start thinking about what he wanted. Or, rather, what he could have.

He released her wrist and nodded toward the cottage. "Can we finish this discussion later? Dragon-shifters have supersensitive hearing, and if we keep going at it, my sister might hear us and flee out the back door."

Melanie's expression relaxed a little. "She's that skittish?"

He nodded. "Yes. I don't make promises lightly, but after our visit with Arabella, I promise you we'll sit down and have a proper chat about you, me, and the baby. For now, can we just put it aside and see how my sister is doing?"

Mel's eyes searched his before she said, "All right, but if you break your promise, Tristan MacLeod, so help me, I will find a way to tie you down and get some answers."

He fought the urge to smile, but couldn't resist. He shook his head. "You might be a good foot shorter than I, and quite a few stone lighter, but somehow I think you'd find a way to accomplish that if you put your mind to it."

Melanie raised her chin. "Of course I would. Everyone told me I wouldn't be able to save my brother, that my odds of qualifying to be a sacrifice would be too great. Yet here I am, while Oliver is finally healthy and out of the hospital."

He couldn't help but tease her. "So through sheer force of will you made your DNA compatible? Somehow I doubt it."

Melanie gave a shy smile and his dragon crooned at the same time his heart skipped a beat. He'd always found her attractive, but the shy smile made her look pretty and vulnerable at the same time. That made him want to haul her against him and protect her all the more.

But he didn't have time for that right now. He motioned with his head toward the cottage. "Come, let's catch Arabella before she disappears."

She nodded and walked the short distance in silence. Apparently, the human could listen to something he said if she wanted to.

Once they arrived at the cottage, Tristan motioned for Melanie to stand off to the side. Then he took a deep breath and knocked on the door. He only hoped Arabella hadn't already fled out the back.

SACRIFICED TO THE DRAGON

~~~

Melanie stood a few feet off to the side of the door and tried not to be selfish and wish Arabella wasn't home. She did truly want to meet Tristan's sister, but a part of her wanted to see if she could get the dragonman to tease her again, as he'd done a minute ago.

Her intuition that the version of Tristan she'd seen with the children was the true one had all but been validated. He could be decent when he tried.

The question was, could he act that way all the time around her? And why did she want to try to find out if he could?

To be honest, she didn't know. Or, rather, deep down she knew why she wanted him to act like that around her, but she wasn't about to get her hopes up. Caitriona had admitted to being that way once, and Melanie didn't want to end up the same way. True, she could never be as reclusive or shy as Cait, but it would be all too easy to lock her heart against any other dragon-shifter, especially since she had yet to meet one who compared with Tristan MacLeod's ability to sear her skin with a touch, or make her instantly wet with a kiss. The man did things to her body she'd never dreamt could be possible outside of a book.

As Tristan knocked on his sister's door, Melanie put her hopes and wishes aside. She didn't think Tristan had exaggerated his sister's pain, and if there was a way to help ease it, she would find it. Somehow, she knew winning over Arabella MacLeod would determine how her future would play out with Tristan.

After knocking for about twenty seconds, the door opened a crack. Melanie couldn't see anything from where she was standing, but Tristan leaned toward the crack and whispered something she couldn't hear. Then the door slammed shut and

Tristan ran a hand through his hair. Melanie was about to ask what had happened, but he put up a hand for her to remain silent.

This time, Tristan didn't bother to knock. He merely shouted at the door. "Arabella Kathleen MacLeod, open this door or I'll break it down. The mother of your niece or nephew isn't feeling well. Are you really going to make her stand out here in the wind and quickly chilling air? I might even scent a storm on the rise."

Wow. As she glanced up at the cloudless sky, she realized that Tristan knew how to lay it on thick.

At first, she thought it wouldn't work. But then she heard the lock click. Tristan turned the doorknob and slowly opened the door.

He took one step inside and said something in that language she couldn't understand. However, it didn't irritate her this time. For all Melanie knew, Arabella might hate English because of the dragon hunters who'd harmed her all those years ago.

The musical syllables of the dragon language stopped and Tristan turned back to her and said in English, "Can you come to the door but not enter quite yet? Ara wants to assess you before letting you into her house. I told her you were one of the good humans, but she is unconvinced."

Her heart skipped a beat at his words. After all, Tristan had just admitted she was one of the good humans.

Before Melanie could reply, a woman's soft yet sharp voice said in English from behind the door, "Belittling my judgment isn't going to help you, Tristan MacLeod."

Mel bit back a smile and decided it was best to approach the door without saying anything. Tristan still blocked the doorway, so she stopped beside him and waited. He reached out a hand as if to touch her, but then he lowered it before he could make contact with her arm. He stepped aside and Mel decided not to let his almost-touch bother her.

She took a deep breath and moved into the doorway. At first, all she saw was the outline of a tall, thin woman. But then the tall, thin woman moved into the light and Mel was careful to keep a faint smile pasted on her face as she got her first glimpse of Arabella MacLeod.

The dragonwoman was nearly as tall as Tristan, probably about six feet, and had the same dark hair and brown eyes. But that was where their similarities ended.

A thick, jagged scar ran from Arabella's right temple, down across the bridge of her nose, and ended near the bottom of her left ear. The right side of her neck was covered in skin that had recovered from a very bad burn; the pink, crinkled skin told her that whatever had happened to Tristan's sister had been painful both at the time and during the long recovery.

But it was Arabella's eyes that Mel noticed most. A mixture of hatred, fear, shame, and sadness shown in them, as if Arabella MacLeod didn't believe anything good would ever happen to her again.

She was on the verge of losing hope.

Tears started to prickle her eyes, but Mel took a second to fight them before she held out a hand and said, "I'm Melanie Hall, Mel to my friends. It's nice to meet you."

Arabella gingerly took her hand, but rather than shake it, the dragonwoman raised it to her nose and inhaled. As soon as she had, she dropped Mel's hand as if it had burned her and looked at Tristan. "The human female is carrying your child. That is the only reason I will let her in here. But if her behavior makes me suspicious, you will leave. Those are my terms."

Mel glanced over at Tristan, and he nodded at his sister before giving Mel a reassuring look, as if to tell her she'd done well so far.

She had no proper training when it came to dealing with survivors of tragedies, so she decided to fall back on her anthropology training. She would observe Arabella and her surroundings to find out what she could without talking to the dragonwoman directly. At least, until she could figure out how to deal with the woman's less than cheerful past and her hatred of humans.

Tristan's sister melted into the darkness of the corridor.

Standing her ground, Mel waited until Tristan placed a hand on her lower back and said, "Come. Let's go inside."

Mel nodded. Without realizing it, she leaned a little against Tristan's side as the dragonman led her into the cottage. The contact reminded her that if she could deal with Tristan-the-asshole, she could very well deal with his sister. She just needed to figure out the best way to do it.

CHAPTER THIRTEEN

As Tristan guided Melanie into his sister's cottage, he breathed a sigh of relief. His argument for his sister to simply scent the human's skin to find out if he was telling the truth or not had worked.

Unfortunately, his sister's sense of smell was as keen as his own, and she had scented Melanie's momentary sadness as she'd stared into Arabella's eyes. Knowing what he did of the human, he didn't think it had been pity. Rather, he believed it had been sadness at what had been done to his sister all those years ago.

Arabella, however, would think the worst of Melanie unless she found a way to change his sister's mind. Not that he should be surprised. Tristan had acted the same way, and a very small part of him was starting to feel slightly guilty about it.

Melanie leaned against him as they made their way to the living room, and his dragon surprised him by crooning. His beast was usually quiet around Arabella. While his inner dragon had never told him why, he had a feeling it was in sympathy of his sister's circumstances. After all, her inner beast had been silent since she had escaped from the dragon hunters ten years ago. After arriving on Stonefire's land and shifting into her human-form, Arabella had never again shifted into a dragon.

He had debated telling Melanie that little detail, but had decided against it. Knowing Arabella had all but lost her dragon-half might make the human act in a way counterproductive to Arabella's acceptance. If Melanie knew about his sister's fear of shifting, she would probably push and ask why. The few times Tristan had brought up the topic with his sister, it hadn't ended well. Ara put up with it from him, but would never tolerate it from a human. If anything, it would cause her to hate Melanie more, and he didn't want that to happen.

And yes, as he tightened his grip on the human female at his side, he wanted his sister to accept Melanie. It wasn't just fulfilling his dragon's wishes; Tristan, too, wanted to get to know the mother of his child. She'd spoken fondly of her brother, and while he vaguely remembered his vial of dragon's blood had gone to heal him, he hadn't bothered to find out what had ailed Melanie's brother.

First her brother, then Caitriona, and now maybe even his sister. It seemed that Melanie Hall had a knack of taking care of everyone but herself. Tristan hoped to fix that, especially since his dragon would revel in protecting and taking care of Melanie. Hopefully that would distract his inner beast from wanting to fuck her every ten seconds.

Then he remembered they were in his sister's house and no fucking would be taking place here. He waited for his dragon to protest, but he kept silent. It seemed even his beast had some sense of decorum.

They arrived in the living room and Tristan guided Melanie to the couch. His sister sat in a plush chair on the far side of the room, one of her laptops in front of her. From the corner of his eye, he noticed the human staring at Ara's wall of photos. Before he could explain them, Melanie said, "Arabella, why do you have hundreds of pictures of different doors?"

126

Ara glanced from her computer screen and stared at the human. Tristan kept his silence and was rewarded with Arabella saying, "Because I like them."

His sister went back to working on her computer, but Melanie pretended as if she hadn't seen his sister's cue that the discussion was over. Instead, she got up off the couch and went to the wall covered in pictures of doors. She looked from one to the other until she stopped in front of one that was crooked and a faded blue. "Where did you take this blue, crooked one?"

Ara looked up from her computer again, but this time at Tristan. He crossed arms over his chest and shook his head. No, he wasn't going to answer for her.

She frowned and he wondered if Ara would actually talk to the human.

Then his sister went back to working on her computer, answering his question.

Glancing at Melanie, he wondered what the human female would do next. Giving up was the last thing he expected from her, so he waited to see what would happen.

~~~

Melanie heard the clicking of keys and knew Arabella had gone back to typing on her laptop. She knew this wasn't going to be easy, but not even asking about something that clearly interested Arabella was getting the dragonwoman to talk with her. She was going to have to try a different approach.

Turning around, she found Tristan on the far side of the room with his arms crossed over his chest. He gave her an inquiring look, but she ignored it and turned back to Arabella.

Her dealings with Tristan gave her an idea. Maybe the siblings were more alike than either had acted at first.

Mel went over to where Tristan's sister was sitting, stopped next to her, crossed her arms, and waited.

It wasn't long before Arabella stopped typing and frowned up at her. "Why are you staring at me? If my actions weren't clear enough, I can say it now: I don't want you here."

Melanie took a fortifying inhale and let loose. "I don't like passive-aggressive behavior. If you're going to dislike me, I want you to tell me straight to my face, because as of right now, I have done nothing to warrant such hatred."

Arabella's eyes flashed. "How dare you talk to me like that in my own home. You humans are all the same—you think we dragon-shifters owe you everything." She slammed her laptop closed and stood up. "You're the reason we even have to bring in humans like you to breed. You killed our kind to near extinction, and if that weren't enough, you now use us as magical blood fountains." Arabella narrowed her eyes. "I despise all of you."

Mel raised her chin. "If you're going to tell me that dragon-shifters are purity and innocence incarnate, I'll start laughing right now." She poked Arabella in the arm. "Violence and wars take two sides to complete. Dragon-shifters have fucked up, just as humans have, but blaming each other for what a small minority has done throughout history is a waste of time. After all, we can't change history. We can only create our own."

The pupils of Arabella's eyes flashed to slits and back. "Thanks to your kind, I have no future to look forward to."

"And why not? You seem clever, stubborn, and are attractive. You're a lot like your brother, actually, and if he can find a woman who likes him, I don't see why you can't find someone. If it's a mate you want, you first need to step outside of these walls and talk with people."

Arabella lost a little of her bravado. "No male would want me." Mel opened her mouth, but the dragonwoman spoke first. "Don't try to say otherwise. I hate fake encouragement and pity nearly as much as I hate humans."

Mel was starting to understand what kept Arabella cooped up inside this house.

Maybe she was crazy, but Mel decided to keep pushing. "Do you think I'm really the type of person who gives fake encouragement? If I only cared about my own skin, I never would've goaded a six-foot tall dragonwoman into an argument. So when I give you a compliment, take it. The only reason you think you have no future is because you keep yourself locked up inside this house and in front of a computer. But it's not protecting you, Arabella. It's slowly killing you."

~~~

Tristan couldn't help but think of how Melanie Hall was bloody fantastic. Even with his sister towering half a foot over her, the human had held her ground and given Arabella an earful.

While he didn't think Ara would hurt the mother of his child, his dragon was prowling around his mind, telling him to be careful. They needed to protect their human. Compared to the dragonwoman, she was fragile.

Melanie might be physically fragile, but bloody hell, the woman was strong inside. He'd seen a glimpse of it when she argued with him, but seeing it as an observer rather than a participant put things into a whole new perspective.

Then the human mentioned if a woman could like Tristan, then Ara could find someone too. Was she talking about herself?

Not that he had time to dwell on Melanie's words. Soon her words made Ara's eyes flash to dragon slits and he blinked. Tristan hadn't seen that happen in over a decade. Had he been wrong all these years? Was Ara's dragon-half still inside her somewhere?

When Melanie called Arabella on her shit, Ara's eyes flashed again and his sister said, "Here you are, all proud of yourself for standing up to me, but you're no different than the rest. When I met you at the door, you pitied me like all the others. There's a reason I stay inside this house, and it's because I don't want to have to explain myself to people like you. I have a job and help the clan. Your pity, along with everyone else's, just takes time away from my work."

Melanie shook her head. "You're wrong. I didn't—and don't—pity you. I felt sad for what had happened to you and the pain you must've endured."

Arabella picked up her laptop. "I don't know why I bother to argue with you. This is my house." She looked at Tristan. "I want you two to leave."

While he was her brother, he had to admire how Melanie was handling the situation. Hell, the human had shown him that Ara's dragon-half was still there. Maybe it was time to try to push her. After all, Tristan had coddled his sister for too long out of guilt.

Two days ago, he never would've believed it, but he was going to side with the human. "No, Ara, unless you agree to come over to my house for dinner in the next few days, and stay for at least two hours, we're staying the night and will continue to stay the night until you give in."

He sensed the human's eyes on him, but he focused one hundred percent on his sister. Ara blinked and said, "What?"

"I've recently been told, by more than one person I might add, that I've let what happened to Mum take over my life. And I'm finally starting to see how that hatred and pain has damaged far more than me. I've tiptoed around you for too long, not wanting to take your issues head on because of guilt. Am I sorry for what happened? Of course. Do I think you should hide away here for the rest of your life? No." He took a step toward his sister. "While you were arguing with Melanie, I saw your dragon-side surface. Twice." He took another step toward his sister. "I need to know—have you been lying to me all these years about your beast being silent?"

Ara's confidence faltered a fraction. "Don't ask me about that, Tristan."

He walked until he was standing in front of his sister. Luckily, she didn't try to run away from him. "It's all right, Ara. If you have, I forgive you. But if you keep trying to hide your beast, I fear that you'll go insane. Have you ever shifted because you couldn't control it over the last decade?"

Fear flashed across his sister's face. "Yes."

He put an arm around Ara's shoulders. "It's all right, love. We're part dragon, and it's only natural."

Ara shook her head. "No. No, no, no. If I'm in dragon form, then the dragon hunters will find me. I need to stay in human form so I can keep hidden from them." She looked up at Tristan, her eyes wild and lost to decade-old memories. "I need to push the beast back, deep, deep into my mind. It's the only way to stay safe."

Tristan hugged his sister and stroked her hair, trying to decide what to do. Despite his, and others', recommendations to see Stonefire's equivalent of a therapist, Ara had always refused.

He glanced over and saw Melanie staring at them. Her eyes were honest and open, and he could swear they mirrored the pain he felt right now for his sister. Recalling how Melanie hadn't been afraid to address the issue head on, gave Tristan an idea.

Never releasing his hold on his sister, he pulled out his phone with one hand and dialed Bram's number. When his clan leader picked up, he said, "Bram, Arabella's on the verge of a breakdown. Because of your dragon's dominance, you're the only one she can't refuse to listen to right now. Will you come to her cottage and see what you can do for her?"

The line was quiet a second and then Bram answered, "I wondered when you would ask me, Tristan. I'll be there as soon as I can."

The line clicked off and Tristan guided his sister to the couch.

Chapter Fourteen

Watching Arabella go from the fiery, confident dragonwoman she'd been with her to the barely functioning individual with Tristan made Melanie's heart ache. To hear that the woman had resisted her dragon-half for nearly a decade made her sadness for Arabella only grow larger.

She wanted to help the dragonwoman, but she knew her intrusion right now would only make matters worse. So, Mel decided to do what her dad always did when there was trouble that required waiting around to solve—she would make some tea.

Since Tristan was preoccupied with holding his sister, Mel went to the room opposite she assumed was the kitchen, opened the door, and discovered she was right. As she put the kettle on and searched through the cupboards for teacups and a teapot, she wondered if Bram could help Tristan's sister. If Arabella could only get over her trauma and act like she'd done with Mel, the dragonwoman's personality—especially her stubbornness—would turn everyone's head in no time. Before long, no one would blink twice at her scars or treat her differently because of them. The question was how to convince Tristan's sister that it was not only possible, but also easy to let people in to look beyond the surface.

In that moment, Mel decided she would visit Arabella again whether she wanted it or not and work on convincing the other woman of her self-worth. Who knew, maybe someday Tristan's sister would welcome her into her home as a friend.

Not that it would be easy. But just like seeing Cait give a weak smile had made her heart sing, so would it be to see Arabella strutting around Stonefire's lands as confident as her brother.

Her motives weren't entirely selfless, of course. After all, Arabella would be the aunt of her baby, and she very much wanted Arabella to be a part of her child's life. To do that, Arabella needed to heal.

The kettle clicked off and she put a couple of tea bags into the teapot she'd found in the cupboards before pouring the water. As she let the tea bags steep, she leaned against the counter and tried not to think about the other major thing that had just happened in the other room. Mainly, Tristan's acknowledgment about his hatred of humans clouding his judgment. Well, it'd been an almost-admission and she'd take it as such.

Between that and the way he'd followed her example of using a direct approach with Arabella rather than dismissing it, a small, very small, part of her started to think she and Tristan might have a chance at a future together. If he could look past the fact she was human and simply try to get to know her, maybe their sexual attraction would become something more. Not that she didn't love the fact he was attracted to her, but there was more to Melanie Hall than her body or ability to breed children.

She sighed. She needed to be careful about wishing for fairy tale endings because it would be dangerous to hope for too much too soon. They hadn't even sat down to talk about what would happen with their child.

She placed a hand on her lower belly. Would he try to take him or her away from her? At one time, she might've thought so. But after today, she was starting to think differently.

Focus, Hall. All of that would have to wait because, first things first, she needed to make sure Arabella was okay.

She splashed some milk into the cups before picking up the teapot and pouring the tea. Once they were full, she carefully picked up the mugs and maneuvered them out into the living room. As she set them down on the coffee table in front of the couch, she felt Tristan's eyes on her. She geared herself up for another possible battle with the dragonman when he surprised her by saying, "Thank you."

Looking up, her heart skipped a beat at the sincerity in Tristan's eyes. She wasn't quite sure what to make of his being nice to her.

However, right now wasn't the time to press him on it. That conversation was something she'd like to do without his sister present. She would wait until after Bram arrived and she could get him alone.

For now, she acted as if he said thank you to her on a daily basis. "You're welcome. I didn't know if you took sugar, so they're just tea and milk."

He raised an eyebrow. "For someone with a not-quite British accent, you act British in a pinch."

Maybe it was selfish, but she very much wanted to have a normal conversation with Tristan without him growling or glaring at her.

She darted her eyes toward the dragonwoman to make sure her condition was unchanged, but Ara was still leaning against Tristan's shoulders with her eyes closed.

Right. If there was anything else they could do to help Arabella, Tristan would've done it already, so she looked back to Tristan's face and said, "Not that you ever asked, but I'm half

British. My mom's American, and I spent my first eighteen years there."

"Why did you leave?"

She nearly blinked. Tristan MacLeod was asking her a personal question.

She cleared her throat. "At first, it was to go to university here. But later we found out that my brother had cancer. So my dad transferred us to the UK so we could both be close to his family and to avoid going into medical-related bankruptcy. Americans don't have a national health service, you know."

"Dragon's blood can't cure cancer. So what happened to your brother?"

She decided not to mention it was in her file and just focus on the fact he wanted to know at all. "Oliver, my brother, finally beat the cancer, but his immune system was shot after the chemotherapy and he contracted a CRE infection. Apparently, it's resistant to antibiotics."

He tilted his head. "And that's when you decided to put yourself up as a sacrifice."

"Yes. My brother deserved a chance to live, and I had the power to give it to him. Or, at least, try. Sometimes I still don't believe I'm compatible, let alone that I passed all the tests."

Tristan studied her a moment and then said, "And what do you think now? Do you regret your choice?"

~~~

Tristan held his breath as he waited for Melanie's answer. His dragon went quiet as well, more eager than he to hear what the female had to say. She couldn't leave them. She was strong. She should raise their young. She would be a fierce protector.

Melanie took a sip of her tea and said, "I don't regret it, but..."

He raised an eyebrow. "But what?"

"I think if you provided the sacrifice candidates with more information ahead of time, then they would be less likely to be scared when they arrive. Knowing about things like the mate frenzy—which I know is rare, but still, it can catch a girl by surprise—and the welcoming ceremony. Stuff like that would've helped me set expectations. I might be a bit strong-willed, but to go through what I went through and be an introvert, well, that could crack such a person."

He couldn't help but smile. "A 'bit' strong-willed? Woman, you nearly put Bram to shame."

She grinned and his heart skipped a beat at the same time as blood rushed straight to his cock. If it weren't for Ara needing him right now, he would go over to the human, pin her against the wall, and kiss the ever-loving shit out of her beautiful mouth.

And that was just what his human-half wanted to do with her. His dragon-half was far more interested in caressing her skin, thrusting between her thighs, and making her scream out their name in pleasure. His beast wanted to bury himself in the human to try to forget all about Arabella's hurt and stress. Yes, they needed to fuck her. That would make them feel better. The sadness would go away.

Before he could stop it, an image of Melanie on her hands and knees in the grass, his hands gripping her beautiful, full arse as he pounded into her tight pussy, flashed into his mind.

His dragon hummed. *Yes. We should fuck her in the grass. Soon. She would like that.*

You can't know that.

She'll like it.

His cock was now at attention and one-hundred percent on board with that fantasy, but as his sister moved against his side, he felt guilty and mentally said to his dragon, *Not now.*

He knew his dragon's need for sex was instinctual, and there was nothing he could do about it. Fighting his dragon's instinct tended to make things worse in the end, but he could at least delay this particular battle until after his sister was taken care of.

There was a knock on the door and he focused back on the here and now. That would be Bram, and he hoped his leader could do something for Arabella.

He tried to pry Ara's arms from around his waist, but her arms only tightened around him. He poked his sister in the side. "Let go. I need to answer the door."

She shook her head against his side. "No. I don't want Bram. He'll force me to talk about the dragon hunters or try to talk to my dragon."

With any luck, yes, he would.

Normally, he'd argue with his sister until she gave in, but right now, she was still half-trapped inside her memories. Otherwise, she'd have fled out the back door by now.

He tightened his grip on Arabella to make sure that didn't happen and he looked at Melanie. "Can you answer the door and let Bram in?"

She nodded, set down her tea, and went to the door. He tried his hardest not to watch her arse as she walked, but he failed. He was mesmerized by the full plumpness of her hips as they swayed with each step she took. His dragon growled inside his head to slap her arse and pull her close.

His inner beast said, *Our female will help erase our sadness. Hold her. Squeeze her. Then you'll feel better.*

138

SACRIFICED TO THE DRAGON

Shut it, dragon.

His dragon huffed but went quiet again.

By the time Melanie came into the room with Bram, he had mostly managed to get both himself and his dragon under control. His clan leader kept his distance, but Tristan could see the concern in his eyes for his hurting clan members. "What do you want me to do, Tristan?"

He looked down at Ara and back to his clan leader. "Talk to her and see if you can get her out of her head. Despite what we thought, her dragon-half is still there. I saw her eyes flash to slits twice."

Surprise flashed in Bram's eyes before he studied Arabella with his piercing blue gaze. Tristan hoped his friend was coming up with a plan. If anyone could help his sister, it was Stonefire's leader.

Finally, Bram nodded. "Right. I'll try. But if I can get her away from you, I think it's best for you and Melanie to leave while I work my clan leader magic on her."

Bram was hiding it well as he always did, but Tristan could sense the dragonman's unease and sadness concerning Arabella. He decided to ease the tension in the room. "And by magic, I hope you don't mean your dick."

Bram smiled. "Not that my cock isn't like magic on a stick, but no, Tristan, you have nothing to worry about when it comes to me. After all, I remember Ara as a wee thing. She's like a sister to me."

Tristan smiled and nodded. "Right. Sit on the other side of her and take a hold of her shoulders. She's probably too far gone to run, but I'm not taking any chances."

He waited to see if Arabella would protest, but she must've retreated back into her memories because she didn't so much as move.

Bram sat down. As he squeezed Ara's shoulder, he said, "Arabella, it's me, Bram. It's time to release Tristan, love, and let me and my dragon help you."

Ara tightened her grip around Tristan and said, "No. I don't want your help."

Bram's expression turned determined, into what Tristan called his "I'm not taking your shit" face.

His leader moved his grip to the back of Ara's neck and squeezed. "Arabella MacLeod, I'm not asking you, I'm telling you as your clan leader to let go of Tristan and look at me."

At first, he wondered if Ara was too far gone to recognize the order and dominance in Bram's voice, but she slowly moved her arms, sat up, and looked at Bram, who gave her a nod of approval.

Since Bram still gripped Arabella's neck, Tristan stood up and said to his leader, "Phone me later and let me know what happens."

Bram never took his gaze from Arabella as he said, "I've got this, Tristan. Go."

Trusting his friend to take care of Ara, he turned to face Melanie. She was unusually quiet, and neither he nor his beast liked it. They liked her moving and lively. He needed to get her out of here.

He placed a hand on her elbow and ignored the heat that flared at the softness of her skin against his. "Let's go."

Melanie nodded, and he guided them out of Arabella's cottage and toward his own. It was time to take Melanie home, not to Samira's place, but to his. Neither half of him wanted to let her out of his sight. He only hoped he could control his dragon once they were out in the open. Without Arabella's pain, his dragon would think of nothing but fucking Melanie. The human female wouldn't understand the reason for the need, and for some reason, her opinion of him was starting to matter.

Rather than think too much on that, he guided her out the door and into the fresh air.

~~~

When they were at a safe distance from Arabella's house, Melanie's curiosity couldn't take the silence any longer and she blurted out, "What can Bram do to help your sister that you can't do yourself? You mentioned something about dominance, but I don't fully understand what that means."

"So you didn't find anything in your research over the years about social structures within the dragon clans?"

She looked at him askance. "So you were paying attention to me on the first day. I wasn't quite sure you were, given your level of assholery."

From out of nowhere, Tristan chuckled. It was low and brief, but she loved how his short laugh made the corners of his eyes crinkle and lessen the harshness of his face. It made him even more handsome than when he was all alpha grumpy. Not that he wasn't attractive when he went all caveman—or was it dragon?—in the bedroom, but this was different. This was a side of Tristan she wasn't used to seeing.

This was a man she could see herself falling for.

His face relaxed with a faint smile and he said, "I like you this way better than when you're reserved and quiet."

She raised an eyebrow. "Good, because it seems with you, I can never be reserved, let alone quiet."

His gaze turned heated. "Yes. Even through the dragon-haze, I remember how loud you liked to cry out in pleasure when I made you come."

Warmth shot through her body at the memory of Tristan's heat on top of her. She should feel bad about it considering Arabella was currently battling her own personal hell, but her hormones didn't have a conscience.

Still, she wasn't about to let his heated look derail her. She'd caught him looking at her back in the cottage with his flashing dragon eyes, and now he was doing it again. She knew what he wanted, but she was determined to get some answers before she let him fuck her again.

She cleared her throat. "So will you tell me about what Bram can do?"

His face took on a neutral expression. "Maybe. What do you plan to do with it? If you're just collecting information for that book you want to write, I can't tell you."

She frowned. "No, I just want to know for me. Well, and..." She took a breath and said, "I also need to know what to do with our child. If this 'dominance' thing can be used on humans, I need some advance warning. I'm not going to let our little dragon baby try to pull one over on me."

He looked over at her. His voice was controlled, almost like he was trying to hide some kind of emotion. "So you're staying, then?"

"Yes, Tristan. Provided I survive the birth, I'm staying."

He clenched his fist and his eyes flashed to slits and back. "You're not going to die."

She poked him in the arm. "Not even your level of stubbornness can prevent me from dying just because you say so." He grunted as if he would argue with that statement and Mel decided to steer the conversation back on track. "Now, tell me about how dominance works with the dragon-shifters."

He unclenched his hand and said, "Well, certain dragons are submissive, while others are dominant. Our inner beasts are a lot like animals in that respect. The more dominant ones have cores of steel. Not only that, they have stubbornness and both an inner and outer strength."

That description fit Tristan to a T.

"So how can Bram's dragon help Arabella's?"

"Her dragon was dominant, once upon a time. These days, it's like a ghost. Arabella has convinced her dragon to hide in fear, so when a strong one gives an order, hers will most likely comply."

She frowned. "But she didn't listen to you. And while I'm not an expert, you seem pretty dominant to me."

He smiled. "I guess I should take 'pretty dominant' as a compliment."

As much as she really wanted to, she resisted the urge to stick out her tongue at him. The asshole version of Tristan could return at any time, and she didn't want to provoke him unnecessarily. For now, she was going to push her luck and ask another question. "So is that why Bram is clan leader? Because of his dominance?"

Tristan's eyes moved to look at the hills and mountains in the distance. "Partly. In addition to his dragon's strength, he's a brilliant fit for the job because of his ability to be patient one minute and then stern the next. I don't think I've seen Bram lose his head since he was a teenager. He has massive amounts of control, more than I could ever hope to achieve."

She fought a smile at his admission of a fault. "How was he chosen?"

Tristan looked back at her and raised an eyebrow. "Inquisitive one, aren't you?" She shrugged and he chuckled again. "Fine. I'll humor your anthropologist's curiosity for a little longer."

Before she could think about it, she said in a dry voice, "Don't strain yourself on my account."

He chuckled and Mel loved the fact she could make him laugh. But as quickly as it had come, his laugh and smile were gone. She would definitely need to find a way to bring it back again. She might just make it her own personal challenge.

She nearly faltered at that thought. Since when did she care about making Tristan smile?

Luckily, Tristan's deep voice stopped her from thinking too hard on that question. He said, "When the clan leadership trials opened up right before our last leader retired, the interested dragonmen and women had to pass a series of obstacles in their dragon forms."

"So, like a display of skills, to prove to the clan the dragon-shifter could take care of them."

"Yes. The very last trial is the most important because it tests how well a dragon-shifter can keep control over their dragon when in dragon-form." He looked over at her. "Under pressure, it's easy to let the dragon-half take control and lose your humanity."

Melanie was hungry for more information. "So how do they test that?"

Tristan silently stared, his deep brown eyes assessing her. For a second, she thought he wasn't going to answer. Then he said, "Several clan members attack a candidate, but not before chasing him or her and then playing a series of mind tricks. The test last three days, and it can be quite brutal."

"But necessary."

He gave a look of surprise. "Yes."

She smiled at catching him off guard. She explained, "I've studied what little I could find about the dragons and their history, and a weak leader would be the death of a clan. You're human, but you're also part dragon. The dragon side needs to do what's necessary to protect those they love."

"And it's not always neat and pretty. I would do whatever was necessary to protect our child, even fight a dragon to the death." He stopped walking and faced her. "While I hope it doesn't come to that, does the idea of me doing what's necessary scare you?"

She stopped and looked up into his deep brown eyes. Her gut told her that her answer would be important to her future; mainly, if she would have one with Tristan as maybe something more or not.

Suddenly, the thought of never feeling Tristan's body against hers or to never again argue or stand toe-to-toe with him caused her heart to ache. Whenever she was with this dragonman, she finally felt like herself. No pretense, no putting on her mask, just her. She'd never even felt that way with her own parents.

Add that to what she'd learned of his past on top of his trust in her by introducing her to his sister, Mel decided that if she wasn't careful, she might even come to love him.

But since today was the first time he'd been civil, she was getting her hopes up a little too early. Regardless, she would be honest. "Sometimes, yes, your dragon-half scares me." Seeing his face become shuttered, she crossed the few steps between them and placed a hand on his chest. "But I sort of like it when your dragon comes to the forefront. It's a part of who you are, Tristan, and I don't want you to hide it from me. Ever."

He placed his hands on her waist and pulled her up against him. "Are you saying that for the sake of our child or for yourself?"

She could barely breathe at the feel of his hard body against hers, but she made her mind focus for a little bit longer. She wanted, no needed, to know something before she let him kiss her. And judging by his half-lidded look, he was on the verge of kissing the shit out of her. "Before I answer, tell me this: does your human-half still hate me?"

CHAPTER FIFTEEN

Reaching out and pulling Melanie's soft body up against his had been a mistake. It was taking everything Tristan had to keep both halves of him from ripping off her clothes and losing himself in the curves and valleys of her body.

But then she went and asked him if his human-half still hated her, and his inner dragon roared for him to tell her the truth. *We can't lose her. I need her. Don't chase her away. Find a way to keep her.*

He pushed his dragon to the back of his mind. He wanted his human-half in control when he answered her. Because, as he stared into her searching green eyes, all he could remember was her telling Arabella how wonderful she was, or how she'd kept her cool in front of Bram and the clan at the First Kiss ceremony. Then there was the fact that she never wanted him to hide his dragon-half.

That combination in a human female was rare, and even Tristan was honest enough to admit it. He'd won the lottery when it came to his choice of sacrifice and the thought of her leaving him had the human-half of him saying, "No fucking way."

His dragon gave a rumble before going quiet again. Apparently, his inner beast approved of that sentiment.

Tristan squeezed Melanie's waist, took a deep breath, and said, "No, Melanie Hall, my human-half doesn't hate you. If anything, I'd say the bastard is starting to like you a little too much."

She smiled, but then it faded. Her brows furrowed and she tilted her head. "Now it's my turn to ask if it's for your sake or for the sake of our child's?"

"Both, because right now you're one and the same."

Her eyes widened. "Tristan MacLeod is spouting fancy words? Am I dreaming?"

He growled. "I can say pretty words when I feel the need. It's just that usually I'm too busy arguing with you, you stubborn woman."

She grinned and he felt liked he'd been punch in the gut. Then she ran a hand up his chest until it rested on the side of his neck. The softness of her fingers against his skin sent a jolt straight to his cock.

It didn't take much for this woman to set him off.

As she started to stroke his skin, his dragon crooned.

He noticed the playful glint in Melanie's eye and his human-half pushed back into control just as she said, "There is a time when I never argue, and that involves you, me, and your dragon naked."

His breath hitched at the same time his dragon roared inside his head at the scent of Melanie's arousal. *Take her. Devour her body. She is ours.*

For the first time since meeting Melanie Hall, Tristan wasn't going to argue with his inner dragon.

He lowered his head and kissed her. The instant her lips opened beneath his, he growled, stroked her tongue, the inside of her mouth, and then nipped her lower lip before he drew her closer against his body. When her hard nipples and soft breasts pressed against his chest, his dragon urged for Tristan to let him take control.

But Tristan told him, *No. This time, she's all mine.*

The dragon was almost smug as Tristan fisted a hand in Melanie's long hair and tilted her head for better access. Her taste was fucking incredible. As her hot, slick tongue met his stroke for stroke, he ached to feel that silky, talented tongue caressing his dick.

Melanie moaned into his mouth as he squeezed her plump arse and he released a drop of precum at the sound. Enough was enough. He needed to do a hell of a lot more than kiss her.

He broke their kiss, and whispered, "I need to be inside you, Melanie Hall. Will you let me fuck you under the sky?"

Her pupils dilated and the rush of her scent into the air told him all he needed to know, but he was determined to hear it from her lips.

He raised a finger and traced her bottom lip, and then the top before pressing his finger inside her mouth. She never broke her gaze as she licked his finger before sucking it deep into the wet heat of her mouth.

Yes, he was definitely going to have to let her suck his cock sooner rather than later.

As she pulled harder, he decided it was time to get naked because, bloody hell, at this rate he'd come from her just sucking his finger. He growled, "Say the words, Melanie, so I can toss you to the ground and devour you."

She grabbed his wrist and pulled his finger from her mouth. She leaned in close and said, "Yes, Tristan. Fuck me under the sky."

~~~

Melanie's heart pounded in her chest as she asked Tristan to fuck her. While she'd been turned on during their weeklong marathon of sex, this time, she felt more. This time, she wasn't giving in to prevent the dragonman from harming her or the clan. No, right now, she desperately needed to feel Tristan's hands on her skin to soothe the ache coursing through her body.

But it wasn't just her skin. She also was wet and swollen for him, her clit pulsing and throbbing for attention. It felt like if she didn't have his cock inside her, and soon, she would die.

Tristan glanced around them, took her hand, and said, "Follow me."

She blinked as he half-dragged her along, heading for the nearby patch of trees at the foot of the closest hill-mountain. He pushed through the mini-forest, careful to hold the branches out of the way so that she wouldn't get scratched. The act softened her heart a little. Even when aroused and no doubt battling his dragon for control, Tristan MacLeod was looking after her.

And she liked it.

A few seconds later, they broke into a small clearing and she gasped. Since it was early summer, everything from the grass to the low foliage was a bright shade of green. There was also a little creek bubbling in the distance, lined with what she thought were flowers. The trees made an almost perfect oval shape around the clearing, shading them from all angles but above.

With the hill-mountain rising up behind the trees, it was breathtaking.

When Tristan removed his shirt, she couldn't focus on anything but the corded muscles of his chest, his abs, and his arms as well as his very thick and enticing tattoo. She definitely wanted the chance to trace it with her tongue.

Untying his boots and sliding them off, he moved to undo his jeans. The next second the jeans were on the ground, and since he was commando, he was now very naked and, glancing down at his thick cock curled against his belly, very aroused.

For her.

She wanted to reach out and stroke all the hard, thick inches of his dick, but then Tristan turned around and bent over. She barely noticed him arranging his clothes on the ground. She was far too distracted by his round, sculpted, and very bite-able ass. After he'd soothed the ache pounding between her legs, she was definitely going to nibble every inch of that fine posterior.

Tristan stood up, turned around, and she drew in a breath at the heat in his still very human eyes. "As much as I like your eyes on me, little human, I think it's time for you to put your gorgeous curves on display for me to admire."

He stalked toward her, and within a few strides, stood directly in front of her. "Either take off your clothes or I'm going to rip them off. It's your choice."

Wetness rushed between her legs at the thought of Tristan wanting her so badly that he'd rip off her clothes just so he could fuck her.

But she'd let him do that at a later date. They still had to make it back to the main living community and it wasn't as if she carried around a spare set of clothes in case of lust-related emergencies.

Never taking her eyes from his, she reached down to the button of her jeans, undid it, and then unzipped them. She wished she could just let them fall and be all dramatic, but instead she broke eye contact to shimmy out of them. When she finally had them off, she realized her head was level with Tristan's cock.

The tip glistened in the sun and she leaned over to taste him, but Tristan fisted her hair and tugged gently. With one last look at his huge cock, she reluctantly stood up and looked him in the eyes again. Her disappointment must've shown on her face because he said, "Later, little human. Right now, the instant I thrust into your mouth, I'd come. I want to taste you first."

Her lips parted. If she'd been wet before, she was drenched now.

Reaching over, Tristan traced the sensitive skin of her belly just above her panties. His touch was rough, warm, and possessive; each stroke sent a little shiver through her body.

Tristan stilled his fingers, grabbed the hem of her stretchy shirt and pulled it up over her head. His gaze caressed her breasts, the curve of her belly, and her full hips before looking back into her eyes. "Take off the rest."

While his eyes were still human, his voice was deep and husky. The fact that her semi-naked body could do that to him sent a rush of happiness and power through her body.

After sliding down her bra straps, she reached behind and unhooked the band. As her bra fell to the ground, she let out a sigh of relief. She felt free.

But then Tristan reached out and pinched both of her nipples and she forgot everything else as she cried out, "Tristan."

He continued to play with one taut peak, but he released the other and lifted her heavy breast in his palm. As he kneaded and squeezed, she reached out a hand to his chest for balance. Without it, her legs threatened to buckle.

His voice rumbled when he said, "Shall I keep playing with your nipples, little human, or are you aching for my touch elsewhere?"

Another pinch to her nipple, and all she could do was moan. She wanted his hot mouth on her sensitive skin, but not on her breast.

She might be straightforward with most things, but she had never felt able to do it with sex. Most likely because of the selfishness of the men she'd dated in the past, who'd only cared about their own orgasms and never hers.

As such, she couldn't muster the nerve to ask for what she really wanted—his mouth on her pussy. Instead, she ran one hand down her belly and rubbed her clit through the material of her panties. She whispered, "Here."

~~~

Holy fuck. How he deserved the human in front of him, he didn't know.

The little vixen was rubbing her clit and all but asking him to fuck her pussy with his mouth. He nearly came right then and there as he watched her hand against the thin material of her underwear. He needed to shred that material, toss her to the ground, and brand her taste on his tongue.

His dragon usually didn't bother with foreplay, but at the thought of tasting the sweet honey between the human's thighs, his dragon roared and said, *Now. Taste her. Brand her with our scent there.*

With great effort, he pushed the dragon back. Tristan wanted to take his time, and his dragon was impatient.

He reached down and pushed her hand aside. He ran a finger under her panties and he groaned. "You're fucking drenched for me."

Before she could reply, he thrust a finger into her pussy and Melanie cried out. He gave her a quick kiss and said, "You're so

153

tight and wet, but I want to feel your pussy squeezing my tongue." He removed his finger. "Get naked, lay down on the ground, and spread your beautiful thighs for me."

As she removed her panties, he drank in the sight of her curves. She was much softer and rounder than the females of his people, but he suddenly realized how he now preferred Melanie's body over any other female's. Just one whiff of her scent or a peek at her skin and all he could think about was molding and squeezing her flesh with his hands before licking every inch of her.

And, of course, fucking the shit out of her tight, perfect pussy.

Lying on the clothes he'd spread out earlier to form a makeshift bed, she parted her thighs. He growled at her pink, swollen skin now glistening in the late afternoon sun.

Unable to resist any longer, he kneeled between her legs and ran his hands up her thighs, up the curve of her belly, and back down to squeeze her soft inner thighs. He pushed her legs wider and looked up into Melanie's eyes. Her cheeks were flushed, her pupils dilated, and her lips parted. With her reddish-brown hair tumbling around her shoulders, it hit him just how beautiful his human was.

His dragon growled. *Tell her.*

Without thinking, he blurted out, "You're so beautiful."

She bit her lower lip and his restraint shattered. His dragon was clawing to get free; if he didn't taste her now, his human-half would lose control.

Not bloody likely. His dragon-half had been the first to fuck her. Tristan wanted to be the first to devour her pussy.

He leaned down and licked her slit, reveling in the musky scent and taste of his little human. Merely tracing the seam of her slit wasn't enough, so he thrust his tongue into her and groaned. He lapped like a cat with milk, unable to get enough of her sweet honey, his cock now hard as steel.

Want her. Take her. Fuck her.

Not yet, he said to his dragon as he thrust his tongue deep in her pussy before retreating to focus on her clit. As soon as his tongue made contact with her slick, hard nub, Melanie moaned and tightened her thighs around his head.

He could draw this out, but from the sound of Melanie's moans, he could tell she was close. Besides, he wanted to send her over the edge so he could have time to explore the rest of her body.

His tongue swirled and lapped at her clit. Melanie tried to raise her hips, but he held her down and squeezed them to keep her in place. Then he bit her. Hard.

Melanie cried out and his dragon rumbled in approval at how loud she screamed. Tristan ignored him and thrust his tongue back inside her core, feeling her muscles squeeze and release around him.

When she relaxed and stopped spasming, Tristan took one last drink of her sweetness, and raised his head. Melanie's eyes were half-lidded, her cheeks flushed, and her expression relaxed. His dragon approved of her sated look, but Tristan's human-half was hungry for more.

He ran his hands up her belly, her breasts, and then cupped her face. As he lay on top of her, her softness cushioning him like a caress, he murmured, "That was just the appetizer. Are you ready for the main course?"

CHAPTER SIXTEEN

Melanie could barely think straight. While she'd orgasmed many, many times during her weeklong sex marathon, none of them had compared to the one Tristan had just given her. She didn't know if it was because of her growing feelings for Tristan or the fact he no longer viewed having sex with her as a chore, but instead as something he desired.

But, quite frankly, she didn't care because, holy crap, the man had a talented tongue.

She didn't have time to dwell on what else he could do with that tongue, because after giving her a very hot, possessive look, he crawled on top of her and cupped her cheeks and said, "That was just the appetizer. Are you ready for the main course?"

Despite her recent orgasm, his words shot straight between her thighs. Somehow she found her voice and couldn't resist teasing him. "Do they only teach you corny dirty talk in dragon school?"

Tristan gave her a wicked smile and her heart skipped a beat. "Why, did you want to attend and learn a thing or two?"

The image of her attending a dirty talk class with a group of tall, gangly teenage dragon-shifters made her laugh out loud.

He nuzzled her cheek and her laughter died as she drew in a breath. She loved the feel of his late-day whiskers on her skin.

But she was having too much fun with her dragonman and she wanted to tease him some more in case he retreated into his gruff self once they both had their clothes back on again. "No, but maybe you could teach me."

Tristan growled and he ended her chance to tease him further by taking a rough kiss. Opening to him, she savored the feel of his hot, silky tongue against hers. He moved one of his hands to her ass and squeezed, his touch like a brand on her skin.

She wanted, no needed, to feel more of his skin against hers. She wrapped her thighs around his hips, grabbed his shoulders, and tilted her hips in invitation. She wanted to feel him inside her.

As she rubbed against him, Tristan snaked a hand between them to pinch one of her nipples and then twist. The pleasure/pain made her cry out. Tristan took the opportunity to kiss her jaw, her neck, and then her shoulder. When he moved down her body, she put a hand on his head and forced herself to speak, "No, Tristan. I want your cock this time."

He looked up. While she saw no sign of his dragon, his gaze was intense. He eased down some more, but before Melanie could work up the nerve to ask him again, he caressed her round belly with both of his hands before he placed a gentle kiss on her lower abdomen.

He was acknowledging their baby.

Her heart squeezed at the action. Tristan MacLeod could be gentle when he tried.

Moving back up to her face, he took her lips as he thrust his hard, long cock inside her. The sudden intrusion was slightly painful, but in a way that was unbelievably good.

Tristan remained motionless, and while she still felt full, she adjusted, her pussy clenching his cock tightly. Her body remembered the way he filled her up, as if he was the perfect fit for her body.

He broke their kiss, looked into her eyes, and said, "This time it's for us and not for the sake of the contract, okay?"

His fierce and tender look, combined with his words, made her eyes grow misty. Rather than risk her voice cracking, she merely nodded.

Growling, Tristan moved his lower body in slow, long strokes, reaching deep inside her. As his pace picked up, she gripped his shoulders and moved with him, never taking her eyes from his.

His very human eyes.

While his human-half was in control, she knew his dragon-half was there too. She wanted to give his inner beast a reward.

On impulse, she scratched her nails down Tristan's back hard enough to leave a mark. Rather than frown or scold, he growled in approval. "Mark me harder."

The "before Tristan" version of Melanie would've hesitated, but she'd tumbled with a dragon and had survived. So, Melanie scored her nails down his back again. Harder.

Tristan cried out and stilled above her, the cords of his neck taut as he came. Much like before, she could feel each hot jet of semen inside her, and the contact sent her over the edge into her own orgasm.

Shouting Tristan's name, she clutched his shoulders to ride the wave after wave of delicious, blinding pleasure that coursed through her body as her pussy clenched and released her dragonman's hard cock.

Tristan collapsed on top of her just as she started to come down from her orgasm. When he lay fully on top of her, Melanie hugged his body tight, afraid he might leave; the memory of waking up alone in her bed last week was still fresh in her mind.

It was stupid, as she barely knew him, but she wanted to lay like this forever with Tristan's weight and heat a comforting blanket. Despite being out in the open and completely exposed, she felt safer than she had in a long time. On an instinctual level she understood that her dragonman would protect both her and their child with his life.

She hugged him closer to her. They would have to uncouple, get dressed, and return to the main living community soon. But for right now, she wanted to pretend they were the only two people in the world. And that maybe, just maybe, she could have more of this, both the sex and the teasing, again in the future.

~ ~ ~

Tristan lay on top of Melanie and finally released the rein on his inner dragon. He expected the beast to demand they flip the human over and take her from behind, rough and hard like during the week of the mate claim frenzy when his dragon had been in charge. But to his surprise, the dragon merely stretched out and hummed in contentment at the feel of the female's skin next to theirs.

Tristan resisted a frown. He'd had his fair share of women over the years, but never had his dragon been so calm and content after fucking a female in the "human way". His dragon liked it rough, hard, and often. His inner beast's new behavior had to be a result of his dragon's nearly complete attachment to Melanie Hall.

He should be worried by that realization since fully attached dragons rarely looked for another female, even if the female the beast had grown attached to refused them. But on the contrary, Tristan's human-half was starting to want her too. Partly because he thought she'd make a brilliant mother, but mainly because he couldn't stand the thought of another male's hands on her.

In that instant, he wanted to cradle her close against him and stroke her soft skin. He rolled over onto his back, taking Melanie with him until she lay against his chest, and he squeezed her tightly.

Our female. Keep her. Hold her tight.

Tristan was starting to agree more and more with his dragon.

He caressed up and down her back, taking the time to learn the dips and curves of her body. He had yet to kiss every inch of her skin, but he would.

His hand stilled for a second before he resumed stroking his human. Yes, he would have her naked and willing in his bed every night, if he had anything to say about it.

Melanie snuggled into his chest and said, "This is nice."

He laid his cheek against her hair. "I would say it was better than 'nice'."

Melanie laughed, the sound making his dragon preen. They should make her do it again.

But instead of teasing her, he said what he really wanted to know. "Come live with me. I don't want you living with Samira any longer. I will take care of you."

She lifted her head and gave him an assessing look. "Is this your dragon, your dick, or your human-half talking?"

I like her, his dragon crooned.

Tristan agreed. "All three, little human." He moved his hand to her arse and took a possessive grip on her right, squishy cheek. "You belong to me, and I want the entire clan to know it."

She battled a smile. "I should be offended at 'belonging' to anyone, but somehow, I'm not adverse to the idea."

He growled and slapped her arse. "So is that a yes?"

Before she could answer, his mobile phone started ringing and he growled. *Fucking fantastic timing, that.*

Since it could be Bram calling about his sister, he reluctantly rolled Melanie onto her back, sat up, and took his mobile phone from where he'd placed it inside his boot. He saw the call was from Ella, another Stonefire teacher, and frowned. While they sometimes took their classes together on trips, she had no real reason to call him.

Curious to see what she wanted, he clicked the receive button and said, "Hello?"

Ella's voice was filled with worry when she answered, "Tristan, thank goodness I got a hold of you. One of the teenagers had a run in with the dragon hunters and we need your help."

CHAPTER SEVENTEEN

At the ring of Tristan's cell phone, Melanie just stopped herself from swearing out loud. She knew the sound meant the end of their little bubble of sex and teasing. Even if it was only a short call, it didn't matter. Interacting with the other dragon-shifters might snap Tristan back into his grumpy self.

Her fear was only made worse when she heard him say, "Dragon hunters?

She stopped breathing, sat up, and listened with every cell in her body to Tristan's side of the conversation. Would talking about the dragon hunters bring back his hatred of humans? Or, his initial hatred of her? After all, he'd been familiar with his hatred for far longer than he'd known her.

And if, indeed, talking about the dragon hunters undid all her hard work in getting Tristan to give her a chance, Melanie wasn't sure she could start all over again. She wasn't about to trap herself into a repeated cycle of niceness and hate. Even her resolve and stubbornness had limits.

Tristan kept his gaze away from her face as he finally said into the phone, "I can be there in forty-five minutes. Contact Kai and Zain to start putting together a rescue plan. But whatever you do, make sure the boy's parents are watched at all times. The last thing we need is for them to go looking for the dragon hunters themselves."

A few seconds later, Tristan clicked off his phone and stared at it. Melanie burned with curiosity, and decided to dare a question. "What happened?"

She steeled herself for a gaze of hatred, but when Tristan's eyes met hers, they were neutral.

His look filled her with a small sense of relief. There was still a chance this could work between them.

He said, "One of the teenagers went out flying on his own into one of the restricted areas and had a run in with a group of dragon hunters."

Melanie's heart clenched. "Is the young one okay?"

"From what information we have, he's still alive." Breaking eye contact, he stood up and reached for his clothes as he said, "Get dressed. We need to head back."

As she watched him pick up his shirt, she made a split second decision and said, "Shift into your dragon form and fly back. That way you can do whatever you need to do to help the teenager faster."

He looked over at her. "I can't leave you alone."

While it wasn't a declaration of love, Melanie felt a small sense of relief at his concern. She still couldn't tell how the news of the dragon hunters had affected him, but he didn't seem to completely hate her. "If you lend me your cell phone, then I'm sure Bram's number, as well as a few others, are in there. I can also call Samira to meet me and take me back to her house." She saw his frown and quickly added, "Just for now. I still want to live with you, Tristan, if you still want me after this."

Rather than give a gushing dialogue about how he couldn't imagine living without her, he merely grunted and said, "I don't like handing over your care to someone else."

She stood up and took a step toward him. "Look, as much as I enjoy your bouts of alpha to the tenth power, if you think I'm going to spend the rest of my life coddled and locked away, then you have no idea who I am." She still didn't see any emotion in his eyes. She took another step toward him. "If I need your help, I will ask for it. But I can damn well handle walking a mile to my friend's house, in the middle of dragon territory no less, unless you're going to doubt the safety of our clan's lands?"

There was a flicker in his eyes, but it was gone before she could tell what it was. After a long moment, he nodded. "Very well. But if I come back to find that you wandered off or got yourself killed, I will bring you back to life so I can kill you myself."

His words still didn't tell her anything about how the phone call had affected him. For all she knew, he just wanted to ensure his unborn child's safety.

She ignored the flash of sadness at that possibility. Not that she didn't want to protect their child, but she wished he wanted to protect her too.

Enough. She wasn't about to turn into someone waiting around for a man to like her.

She raised her chin and placed her hands on her hips, not caring that she was standing naked with unruly hair in the middle of an outside clearing. "Again, your stubbornness isn't quite that powerful, but I suppose I can live with that threat."

She looked around the clearing. While she hadn't seen Tristan in his dragon-form yet, she bet he was at least as big as those two dragons she'd seen on her very first day on Stonefire's land and neither of them would fit here. She said, "Will you be able to fit if you change in the clearing?"

SACRIFICED TO THE DRAGON

~~~

Tristan stared at Melanie and tried not to let his mixture of emotions show on his face. He had no right to blame the human female for what was happening to Miles, the teenager that had been captured, but some of his hatred of humans was seeping back into his consciousness. The sooner he could take care of the problem with Miles, the sooner he could spend more time with his female and work on ridding himself of his hatred for good.

Especially since his dragon was determined to keep her.

While he'd grudgingly agreed to let her return on her own, something his dragon was very much not happy with, now she was asking him about shifting and fitting into the clearing. He shook his head. "No, but you can get dressed and wait here for Samira. I'll go beyond the trees where there's more room and shift there."

Melanie's lips pressed into a thin line and then she said, "So you trust me enough to fuck me in the open, but not enough to allow me to see you shift into a dragon."

Her tone ignited his temper. "I'm not a bloody mind reader. You didn't even ask if you could watch me."

She blinked. "Well, then, can I?"

"No."

She closed the distance between them and punched him in the chest. "Good to see the asshole version of Tristan MacLeod has returned. I was starting to think you might be a nice guy under all that alpha anger."

With her eyes blazing and her cheeks flushed, all he could think about was how much he wanted to kiss her. But he pushed that thought aside. "Again, you're jumping to conclusions." He grabbed the wrist of her hand still on his chest, her touch burning his skin. "Humans don't handle seeing the shift well. And if this is to ever work between us, the last thing I need is for you to think of me as a monster."

At that, Melanie blinked. Her voice was no longer angry when she said, "After all of this, you still think I fit the stereotype of a typical human? When will you start thinking of me as Melanie Hall and not just 'a human'?"

His dragon said, *Stop it. She is ours. She is different. Tell her.*

But Tristan denied his dragon. That conversation would have to wait. A teenage dragon-shifter needed his help.

Still, both halves of him wanted to feel her softness one last time before possibly taking on a group of dragon hunters. While he shouldn't have to attack anyone since he wasn't one of the clans' trained Protectors, anything could happen.

He reached out and pulled her flush up against him. As the womanly scent that was Melanie filled his nose, a scent with a slight undertone of himself because of their baby, he decided this woman deserved a chance to watch him shift.

Over and over again she'd proven she was different, so it was time to see if she could pass the ultimate test. He said, "Give me a kiss and I'll allow you to watch me shift."

She raised an eyebrow. "You'll 'allow' me to watch? When you get back, Tristan MacLeod, we're going to work on your domineering tendencies."

Despite everything that was going on, he smiled. "There's my little human, full of spirit. Now, kiss me and watch me shift."

For a second, he wondered if she would acquiesce. Then she raised her face. "You kiss me and then I suppose I can watch you shift."

His dragon loved that this human kept challenging him. *She will make a fine mother for our young.*

Tristan lowered his head and took her mouth in a demanding kiss. He squeezed her arse as his lips swept against hers, her taste making him growl. He had wanted the entire afternoon for him and his human, but it wasn't to be.

At least now he had a bloody good reason for coming back alive from the rescue attempt. He had many more dirty things to do to his female while his human-half was in charge, and even more creative ideas from his dragon-half.

He gave her one last swipe of his tongue before he retreated, bit her lower lip, and said, "Toss my shirt over you. It'll dwarf you since you're short, but it's the quickest way to hide your nakedness from other males."

She smiled at that and pushed against him. He reluctantly let her go and watched her walk over to his shirt and bend over. His cock took notice of her full, soft arse in the air and became as hard as steel.

Thankfully, she tossed the shirt on quickly and pulled on her underwear to hide her tempting curves. After reaching over to grab the rest of her clothes, she stood up and said, "There. Now I'm covered in your scent. I'll keep it on until you get back. Will that satisfy both you and your dragon?"

Yes. Ours.

Tristan nodded, walked over, and handed her his mobile phone. After she tucked it into the pile of her clothes and shoes at her chest, he took her hand. "Now, come with me so I can shift and go help the teenager."

He thought he saw sadness flicker across her face, but it was gone before he could be sure. Was his human female growing attached to him as well and sad because she didn't want him to leave? His dragon crooned at that idea, and his human-half was more pleased than he would've guessed.

He tugged her gently behind him. When they reached the tree line, he dropped Melanie's hand and scooped her up. She let out a noise of surprise, but he wasn't sure why. It wasn't as if he would allow her bare feet to become scratched by the fallen debris.

For once she didn't argue and just curled up against his chest. He squeezed her tighter with his arms, as if to reassure himself that she was safe. He trusted the other Stonefire dragon-shifters not to harm her, but there were more than a few who despised the human female sacrifices. They could make her sad with words, and he growled at the thought.

Melanie looked up. "What was that for?"

He shook his head. "Nothing."

Her eyes were skeptical, but she didn't question him. Not that she wouldn't do it later, but he reckoned she wanted to save the young dragon-shifter as much as he did and didn't want to waste time arguing.

The brief flash of hatred that had coursed through him at the news of Miles' capture faded. Melanie Hall would never be like the barbarous poachers who hunted his kind. Her heart was too soft for betrayal or deceit.

And for the first time, he started to realize how much of a bastard he'd been to the big-hearted woman in his arms.

Guilt was a distraction, so he pushed it aside. He needed his brain to focus on the upcoming take down and rescue operation. He could make it up to his female later.

He made his way through the trees, careful not to allow Melanie to get scratched by any of the branches. Within two minutes, they were back on the open landscape of the area. He set her down and said, "Stay here. I need more room to shift."

Sacrificed to the Dragon

As he walked away from her, he started to feel something he hadn't felt in a long time—nerves. Tristan was nervous.

So far, Melanie Hall had been understanding about the dragon-shifters and their ways, but could she handle him changing into a dragon? Some humans found dragons beautiful, but a much larger portion saw them as monsters.

She won't be afraid. She is strong.

He decided to listen to his dragon. Once he was about ten feet away from Melanie, he stopped and turned around to face her. Her gaze was curious and a touch impatient, which was a hell of a lot better than scared or nervous.

Hurry, his dragon urged.

Right. The teenager. They needed to save the young. Delaying his shift wasn't going to help anyone or change the way Melanie would look at him after this.

Tristan closed his eyes and let his dragon into the forefront of his mind. As he imagined his body merging with his dragon's, a low hum of pain sizzled through his bones, signaling he was about to shift.

It was time to see what his human was made of.

~ ~ ~

Melanie watched Tristan walk away from her and it took everything she had not to run after him and jump back into his strong, muscled arms. Given the chance, she could revel in his heat while breathing in his spicy male scent for days and still not get enough.

Her dragonman's touch was becoming addictive, and she didn't think it was just because he was the father of her unborn child. No, she knew it was because she was growing to love it.

But to act on her impulse would be selfish. She wasn't about to cost a teenage dragon-shifter his life.

Instead, she contented herself by lifting the collar of Tristan's shirt she now wore to her nose and inhaling deeply. If his scent wasn't enough to make her feel good, then his shirt, which dwarfed her despite the extra padding she carried on her hips and ass, did. It reminded Mel of how Tristan made her feel small.

How he made her feel desired and feminine.

Before her thoughts could keep wandering down that path, Tristan stopped about ten feet away and faced her. His eyes were unreadable and she wished she knew why.

But then he closed his eyes and she stopped fingering his shirt to watch as his hands turned into claws with talons, his arms elongated, his nose turned into a snout, and wings sprouted from his back. His skin gradually turned black as scales appeared to form his dragon's hide. In less time than it took to say Mississippi five times, he was a fifteen-foot tall dragon with shimmering black scales and piercing brown eyes.

Slitted eyes that were looking straight at her.

For a second, her heart rate ticked up. Seeing a dragon up close was a little more intimidating than she'd imagined. As the dragon opened his jaw a little, she could see his long, sharp teeth.

Teeth that could shatter her arm in the blink of an eye.

But as the dragon continued to stare at her, she realized she'd seen those eyes before, whenever Tristan's dragon-half had been in control.

And the dragon's eyes weren't fierce or threatening. She might not be a dragon body language expert, but if she were to hazard a guess, she would say Tristan in dragon-form looked uncertain.

SACRIFICED TO THE DRAGON

No doubt, it was because of her.

The fact that her strong, alpha dragonman was vulnerable right now went straight to her heart. She needed to erase his doubts and convince him of how beautiful he was with the sun glinting off his scales and half-raised wings. Someday, she hoped he would allow her to touch those wings and see if they were as smooth as they looked.

Confident her dragon wouldn't hurt her, Melanie took one step and then another, giving Tristan plenty of time to jump and fly away if he felt he was a danger to her. She may not know everything about him, but she knew deep in her bones that Tristan MacLeod would never willingly harm her. Even if not for her sake, then at least for the sake of their child.

But the black dragon stayed put. When she was close enough, Tristan lowered his head and bumped his snout against her shoulder. Not hard, or she would be flying across the clearing, but enough to make her lose her balance and grab onto the dragon's snout to stay standing.

Once she was solidly standing on two feet again, she dared to stroke Tristan's nose. To her surprise, his scales weren't slimy or sleek, but rather felt like hard, grooved leather.

Taking a deep breath, she finally looked into her dragon's eyes. They were huge and a deep sepia brown, the color reminding her of dark, unpeeled potatoes.

Okay, that might not be the most romantic description in the world, but she still loved the deep color and slitted pupils of the dragon in front of her. Hell, she would love any color as long as it belonged to her dragon-shifter.

She didn't know how long she stood there staring into her Tristan-slash-dragon's eyes, but the dragon let out a chuff of warm air. The feeling against her skin snapped her out of her trance and she said, "Right. You need to leave."

She placed her hands on either side of the dragon's wide jaw and stroked. The dragon started humming and she smiled. Then she remembered what she wanted to say.

Putting on a stern expression, she said, "You come back to me alive, Tristan MacLeod, or I will be the one to bring you back to life just so I can kill you."

She was convinced there was laughter in the dragon's eyes and she grinned. On impulse, she kissed the dragon's snout, gave him one last pat, and stepped back. "Now, go rescue that boy and show those dragon hunter bastards that it's idiotic to mess with a Stonefire dragon-shifter."

The dragon nodded, turned, and jumped into the air. Watching what had to be at least twenty-five thousand pounds of muscle and wings ascend into the sky was a beautiful sight to behold. All too quickly, Tristan was gone.

Rather than worry about what the dragon hunters might do to him, Melanie decided to put her faith in Tristan. Besides, there wasn't anything she could do to help him. Well, she could get her ass to Samira's place and eat something. The little dragon-shifter baby inside of her uterus was making her hungry.

Melanie took out Tristan's cell phone and dialed Samira's number. Her friend answered on the second ring. After arranging for Samira to come get her, Melanie hung up the phone, put on her jeans, socks, and shoes, and sat down on a nearby boulder.

Now, all she could do was wait.

Chapter Eighteen

Forty-five minutes later, Tristan and two of his clan members were on their way to where Miles had last been seen, according to the boy's friends.

Two of Stonefire's Protectors, Kai and Zain, flew on either side of him. The clan's highly skilled Protectors were tasked with getting Miles out alive, but it was Tristan's job to make sure the boy's inner dragon could be contained and brought under control.

Or, if worse came to worse, to try to coax Miles' inner dragon enough to ensure the boy didn't try to commit suicide. That was always a possibility when a young dragon-shifter was pushed to emotional and physical boundaries. Not that the dragon hunters would care.

Normally, Ella, a fellow teacher, would be the one to go and wrestle or soothe the teenager's inner beast since she had been his teacher for far longer than Tristan had. But the female dragon-shifter was two months pregnant and she'd decided to avoid angering her mate by sitting this one out.

Not that he could blame her. A male dragon-shifter with a pregnant mate was not something you messed with. He was fast learning that himself.

Tristan's wings missed a beat at that thought. Since when had he started to think of Melanie as his mate? Her being unafraid and accepting his dragon-form was doing strange things to his mind.

If there had ever been a way for her to convince him that she wasn't like other humans, it would be for her to caress his hide while in dragon-form. If that hadn't been enough, she'd then gone and kissed him on the snout.

His dragon-half still hummed at the feeling of her lips against their hide. His inner beast was content to let his human-form take care of their female sexually, but his dragon liked the odd caress or two. Especially since she wasn't afraid of them. Next time, his dragon wanted to lie down and have her lean against him, or maybe have her stroke the ridge of his wing. *Yes, that would feel good. Maybe she would even scratch behind my ears. Dragonhide can be itchy.*

Tristan pushed his dragon back before he started thinking of every way he wanted their female to pet him. His beast was clearly smitten.

Thankfully, the rock formation designating their target destination came into view, and Tristan put all thoughts of Melanie aside. If he didn't concentrate one-hundred percent on this rescue, the teenage dragon-shifter might die.

No. He wasn't about to let that happen.

Per their agreed upon plan, Tristan fell back to allow the two Protectors to the front of their formation as they landed in the clearing near their craggy landmark. Kai nodded to Zain and then shifted from his gold dragon form back into a tall blond-haired, blue-eyed human.

Then Kai jogged to the far side of the clearing and disappeared behind a series of tall rock formations where the two teenagers should be waiting for them.

Sacrificed to the Dragon

Both Tristan and Zain remained alert, but Tristan neither scented any threats nor heard anything unusual. Glancing at the red dragon sharing the clearing with him, Zain was standing on all four legs with his wings slightly extended, but he was relaxed and not tensed to pounce. The other dragon didn't sense a threat either.

A few minutes later, Kai reappeared with two rather scared looking teenage males.

The Protector ushered the two boys toward where Tristan and Zain were waiting in their dragon forms. Once they were about a half-dozen feet away, Kai said, "Okay, lads, tell them what you told me."

One of the teenagers, the one with dark skin and a closely shaved head, darted a glance to Kai and then said, "W—we didn't mean for this to happen. It was just a dare, you see. But Miles wanted to prove he was just as fierce as one of the Protectors. So we set him a challenge—to bring back something with the Carlisle dragon hunters' logo on it."

The Carlisle dragon hunters?

Bloody fantastic. The dragon hunters divided themselves into groups that were the equivalent of a cross between a gang and a motorcycle club, and the Carlisle branch were some of the nastiest and most brutal dragon hunters in the United Kingdom. Maybe even in all of Western Europe.

Provided the boy was still alive, getting him out was going to take some finesse. Luckily, Kai and Zain were the top tier of security for Stonefire and knew a thing or two about getting in and out of dangerous places undetected. Like most other dragon-shifter Protectors, they had spent some time helping out the human military in their early twenties. In exchange, the British military helped to keep the dragon hunters at bay.

Well, at least most of the time.

Eyeing the two teenage boys, Tristan decided to let out a soft growl for good measure, and they cringed a little. Good. Maybe they wouldn't pull this stupid shit again.

Kai said to the boys, "You two are going to stay here while we fetch Miles. If you don't hear from us in the next two hours, you call someone else. Don't try to run off on your own. Understood?"

The two boys nodded and Kai looked up at Zain and Tristan. "The boys hadn't mentioned it was the Carlisle group when they phoned earlier. Our previous plan won't work." Kai's light blue gaze moved to him. "Time is of the essence when dealing with the Carlisle hunters and we can't afford to wait for back-up. Instead of hanging back until we bring the boy to you, you're going to have to fly in with us to rescue him. Are you up for it?"

Tristan lacked the special ops-like training of any of the Stonefire Protectors, but even so, neither his human-half nor his dragon-half would abandon a young to the Carlisle dragon hunters.

He nodded and Kai said, "Good. Here's what we're going to do..."

He listened and hoped he could pull this off. The alternative was him dying and abandoning Melanie and their child for good.

And he sure as hell wasn't about to let that happen.

~~~

Melanie was sitting inside Samira and Liam's cottage, reading a book to Samira's son, Rhys, when a loud sound that could only be called an ear-splitting moan rent the air. Rhys jumped at the cry before cuddling against her chest. The boy was shaking.

As she made soothing sounds and stroked the boy's back, his actions told her that the moan wasn't an everyday sound around Stonefire. She hated not knowing what it meant.

Samira rushed into the room and Mel pounced on the chance to ask her, "What the hell was that?"

Her friend looked worried. "A dragon's been hurt."

Her heart skipped a beat as dread pooled in the pit of her stomach. If it was Tristan that had been hurt…

Stop it. She had no idea if it had been Tristan's cry she'd heard or another dragon's. There was no reason to get upset for nothing.

Forcing her voice to remain steady, she asked the all-important question, "Do you know who made that sound?"

Shaking her head, Samira came over to lift Rhys off Melanie's lap. "No, and I can't leave Rhys or risk taking him with me if there is indeed a wounded dragon. I hate not knowing who it is. Can you go check it out?"

The fact Samira had asked her to go check meant the world to Melanie because sitting around and fidgeting while her man was out doing something dangerous was not her style.

Of course, she still didn't know everything about Stonefire yet and she wasn't about to go out blind. She asked, "How do you know that was a wounded dragon?"

Samira cuddled her son close and her expression went grim. "Believe me, once you hear that sound, you never forget it. A dragon only cries that way when they're close to dying."

The eerie moan sounded off in the distance again and Melanie agreed. The pain and anguish in that cry was something she hoped never to hear again.

What if it was Tristan's cry? No. She wouldn't allow herself to worry. She'd managed to hope for the best with her brother and she could certainly do the same for her dragonman.

Mel stood up. "Where should I go to see what's happening? And is there anything in particular I should know about approaching a wounded dragon?"

Samira studied her a second and then said, "If it's an unknown dragon-shifter, then keep your distance. Often when dragons are wounded, their dragon-halves come to the forefront and are unpredictable, just like a wild animal would act if it was hurt."

"Check. Stay away from the sharp teeth and claws." Mel was just about to turn and get her things when she decided to stop being a coward and ask what was on her mind. She couldn't rule out Tristan completely, and no matter what she found out, it was best to be prepared. If the heart-wrenching cry was indeed her dragon-shifter's, she would need to act fast on arrival.

No matter what it took, if Tristan was hurt, she would find a way to save him. He was too stubborn to die.

She clenched and released her fists to help ease her pent-up worry. Then she took one last fortifying breath and spit out, "And if it's Tristan? What can I do then?"

"For your sake, I hope it's not Tristan. If it is, you more than anyone have a chance at calming him down enough to let the healers do their work."

"Because of our child?"

"No. Because his dragon is attached to you. Talk to him and try to find a way to let him sniff your skin, and the dragon should calm down. Hurting you would destroy both halves of Tristan."

While she didn't want to admit it, this wasn't the time to rule out all possibilities. She whispered, "And what if I can't find a way to calm him down?"

Sadness flashed in Samira's eyes. "Then Tristan might die. For all that dragon-shifters are powerful creatures, when they're injured and their human-halves lose control, it's hard to heal them. That's the single biggest cause of dragon deaths apart from old age."

"Talk about pressure."

Samira gave a weak smile. "It may not be him, so don't stress yourself out beforehand. It's not good for the baby."

For a second, Melanie had forgotten about her baby. But no matter what, if it was Tristan, she would find a way to help him, pregnant or not. She didn't want to live without him.

Wait a second, where had that come from? She barely knew the man.

Stop lying to yourself. Between the instant he'd allowed her to see him shift to when she'd kissed his long dragon snout, she'd realized that she could never be with anyone else. Tristan was hers, and she would fight for him if she had to.

"I'll be as careful as I can, but I won't abandon him, Samira. I can't do it."

Her friend shifted her son to her other arm. "I hope Tristan realizes what he has in you."

I hope so too. But she didn't want to have that discussion right now. She needed to find out which dragon was injured, and stat. "Where will they take the hurt dragon?"

"There's an emergency surgery next to the main landing area. The dragon would be there."

179

Another moan pierced the air, shooting straight to her heart. She couldn't afford to waste any more time, so Mel nodded. "Right. I'll let you know what I find out."

She then turned to grab her cell phone and exited the door just as another cry pierced the air. If one sound could ever encompass the epitome of pain, the anguished dragon's cry was it.

~~~

Twenty minutes later, Mel approached the main landing area and couldn't believe how many people were standing near but not too close to it. She hoped it was for support rather than as a spectacle. Dragons were too big to have any sort of privacy when hurt, and she might not be a doctor, but surely the stress of so many nearby couldn't be good for a dragon moaning in pain.

Still, as she looked around the crowd, maybe one of them knew who was hurt. Otherwise it was going to take some creative ideas to get through the throng of tall, strong-ass dragon-shifters.

She'd had about a fifty-fifty success rate when it came to meeting friendly dragon-shifters during her time here. However, she wasn't about to let that deter her. Tristan might need her.

Squaring her shoulders, she took a deep breath for confidence. What's the worst they could do? Call her a whore again?

She went to the nearest female and asked, "Who's been hurt?"

The dragonwoman turned and stared down at her with her piercing brown eyes, her expression unreadable. The woman may tower over her, but Mel wasn't going to be intimidated. Especially not when Tristan's life could be at stake.

SACRIFICED TO THE DRAGON

The woman finally gave a sad smile and Mel's stomach dropped as the dragonwoman said, "You are quite the brave one, human. Normally, I'd like to see what else you're made of before giving out information, but I'll make an exception in this case." She gestured toward the landing area. "Go. Your Tristan is dying."

Her heart skipped a beat. *No.* It couldn't be true. Tristan was strong and brave, to an unbelievable alpha degree. He couldn't be dying.

Mel turned toward the crowd. She'd just have to find him and convince his stubborn ass to fight for his life.

She searched out a path to the landing area and for once wished she had wings so she could fly over all these people. However, before she could ask anyone to move out of the way, the woman behind her yelled something in the dragon language. All eyes went to Melanie. Gone were the looks of contempt, disgust, or curiosity. Instead, they were now eyeing her with varying degrees of sadness and pity.

That definitely wasn't good news.

Tears threatened to fall, but she forced them back. *Get it together, Hall. You can't help him if you turn into a blubbery mess.*

As a path magically cleared for her, she kept her head high as she half-ran, half jogged toward the landing area. She wasn't in the best shape, but she ignored the shortness of her breath and kept up her pace. She wasn't about to let a little thing like being overweight stop her from reaching her man.

Besides, Bram hadn't tried to contact her, and if Tristan were truly dying, he would have.

For now, she had to believe that rumors about her dragonman were inflated. After all, gossip tended to do that to the truth.

She only hoped that was the case this time because if Tristan was dying, she might not be able to keep herself together. She'd not only start crying, but her heart would break. Not just because her baby would be without a father, but also because she would miss the odd combination of his grumpiness and his tenderness.

Please, Tristan, hold on for me. I'm coming.

CHAPTER NINETEEN

Pain. Blood. Death.

Those three words repeated themselves over and over inside Tristan and his dragon's head. Tristan's human-half was weak, and the dragon-half had taken control, which meant his beast had fallen back on instinct.

The human part of him was vaguely aware of the other dragon-shifters trying to help him, but his dragon-half was snarling and whooshing its tail through the air to keep everyone away. His dragon roared inside their head. *They will pounce on our weakness. They will kill us. I must keep them away.*

No, they want to help us. They will heal us, he shouted at his beast. But his words fell on deaf ears.

He tried to muster the strength necessary to push his dragon back, but none of the tricks every dragon-shifter learned as a child had any affect on his beast's pain-induced rage. Not even Tristan's stubbornness was working. Due to the gaping, bleeding wounds on his chest and shoulders, Tristan's usual inner strength was all but gone.

Yet if he couldn't get control of his dragon, he would die.

All of the sudden, an image of Melanie naked in the grass, her gorgeous, pale curves on display and her eyes full of stubbornness, came into his mind. In his vision, she was rubbing her clit and beckoning him to thrust his long, hard cock inside her.

It was strange the things that came into your mind when you thought you were dying.

But then remembering Melanie also brought back the fact he might never see his child.

He tried to use the loss of Melanie and their baby as a way to garner the dragon-half's attention, and for a second, he stilled. Then his beast's pain-induced fit started up again and Tristan mentally let out a frustrated sigh.

If only he could see Melanie one last time. Maybe then he could find the strength to push his inner beast back and have a chance to survive. Not just for their baby, but for her as well. In this moment he wasn't about to lie to himself. He cared for his little human.

However, she had no way of knowing he was injured, and even if she did, it was nearly too late. If he didn't receive the attention he needed within the next thirty minutes, he would die.

Even then, survival wasn't guaranteed.

Another group of healers approached him. His dragon snarled at them and then knocked two of the dragon-shifters flat on their arses with his tail. Three more dragon-shifters tried to approach him from a different direction, but Tristan knew their chances of success weren't going to be any better;

a dragon in pain would use up any and all strength to keep away perceived threats.

Before his three clan members were close enough to swat away, his dragon moaned into the air again. The constant, throbbing pain confused the beast. He wanted it to stop.

Even in the midst of his frustration with his dragon, he couldn't help but try to send soothing thoughts.

Then all of the sudden the healers turned and ran toward an oncoming figure. If his dragon would only stretch its neck, Tristan could see who had come. If not Melanie, then he hoped Bram. His clan leader had a better chance at helping him than the current group of nearby dragon-shifters in the landing area.

But with the other dragon-shifters gone, there was no threat and his dragon laid his head down on the ground and struggled to stay awake. His beast's voice was weak inside his head. *Sleep will bring relief and the pain will vanish. I can make all the pain stop.*

Stay awake, dragon. Tristan knew that as soon as his dragon fell asleep, that would be it. He wouldn't wake up again.

In a last burst of strength, Tristan shouted at his dragon. *We need to stay awake. If you fall asleep, we'll never see our human again. Never hold her. Never fuck her. Never stand by her side as she births our young. Don't you want to live to see all of that? We must stay awake or she will be alone.*

But his beast merely ignored him and tried falling asleep again. Tristan used what precious strength he had to battle his dragon-half. Tristan wasn't one to beg, but in this moment, he would do it if it meant he could see Melanie again.

As the last of his energy faded, Tristan tried one last tactic. *If you don't let the healers help us, we will die. There will be no one to protect our female. She needs us.* But his dragon was too far gone to listen to reason.

As his beast closed their eyes, Tristan was out of options. They were going to die.

~~~

A group of dragon-shifters she'd never met before surrounded Melanie. They were all telling her to go home, but she wasn't about to cow down to them. She could hear Tristan's dragon in pain, and the sound only strengthened the steel in her spine.

Putting her hands on her hips, she looked to the dragonwoman directly in front of her. The woman with mousy brown hair tied in a ponytail seemed to be their leader. Melanie would focus on her. "You all haven't been able to help him, have you? So let me try. His dragon is attached to me. Tristan and his dragon would never hurt me."

The ponytailed woman frowned and said, "No. I'm not about to put you or your baby at risk. Bram would have my head."

186

Melanie shook her head and decided if the woman was going to use Bram as an excuse, so would she. "I don't agree with you. Bram would want us to try everything we could to save a clan member. And right now, I'm Tristan's last hope."

One of the males in the group said, "She's right, Cassidy. If he can scent her, he may let her come near."

A few of the other dragon-shifters murmured their agreements and Melanie felt a glimmer of hope in her heart.

Cassidy crossed her arms over her chest and shook her head, and Mel wasn't sure what to think. Then the woman said, "I've done all that is required of me at this point. If you want to get yourself killed by a pain-crazy dragon, then that's your own damn fault. Just make sure he doesn't shift back into a human because doing that right now will kill him." Moving aside, she motioned behind her with her head. "If you understand all of this and accept the risks, then go to him."

Thank goodness. Mel nodded and squeezed between the dragon-shifters, not wanting to waste any more time talking. Once past the circle of dragonfolk, she could see Tristan in dragon-form curled up on the ground, the dragon's eyes closing and then opening again as if he were trying not to fall asleep.

She had a feeling that if the dragon fell asleep, he'd never wake up again.

Mel knew she didn't have long, so she did a quick scan of the dragon to find his injuries and sucked in a breath at the huge gash along one of his shoulders. Thick, red blood dribbled from the shoulder wound and she fought back the vomit threatening to come up. *No, little dragon baby. We're going to help your dad, so buck up.*

With a deep breath, Mel took three more steps toward the dragon and said, "Tristan. It's Melanie. Please. Look at me."

The dragon's eyes fluttered open, but otherwise ignored her.

She didn't like the look in the dragon's eyes, as if he was in such pain that there was no hope of relief. Tristan's human-half would never give up, which must mean he'd lost control. She needed to try again.

She inched another foot closer and decided to screw the gentle approach. That wasn't really how she operated anyway.

She waggled a finger in the dragon's direction and said, "Now listen here, Tristan's dragon-half. You're hurt and maybe dying. If you don't let some of those nice dragon-shifters over there help you, you'll die. And if you die, that means I have to find another nice, handsome dragon-shifter male to take care of me, caress me, and even fuck me. Is that what you want?"

She heard murmurs of "she must have a death wish" behind her, but she focused solely on the dragon.

She was rewarded when the dragon's eyes flicked to hers and she saw a small spark. It wasn't much, but she'd take it as encouragement to keep pushing. She took another step closer and said, "That's right. If you die, then another male's hands will be all over me and another male's cock will be inside me, branding me with his scent. And if that isn't enough, then realize you dying means that another male will raise your young." She turned half away. "If you don't let us help you, maybe I should start looking right now. I passed quite a few hot males on my way here."

The dragon raised its head and growled. Resisting a smile, Mel turned her head back toward the dragon, looked him in the eye, and raised her eyebrows. "Don't like those possible scenarios, now, do you? Well, then, if you want to be the only male who touches this body, then you'd better let the others help you so you can live. To do that, I need you to let your human-half come back into control."

As the dragon continued to stare at her, Mel wasn't exactly sure how she'd know if the dragon-half ceded control or not. But no doubt the dragon-shifters behind her would know if she couldn't figure it out.

She was about to start scolding and taunting again when the dragon's head lowered to the ground and let out a long, slow breath of air. The beast's eyes were no longer frenzied, but rather stoic.

Yes, stoic like Tristan's default expression.

"Tristan," she whispered and barely restrained herself from running to the dragon. She was hopeful, but not stupid. She needed more than an expression to convince her it was safe to approach.

She clenched a hand over her heart, took a steadying breath, and said, "If it's truly you, flick out your tongue."

While there was still pain, something that looked like amusement hovered in the dragon's eyes. Then he flicked out his long, forked tongue and turned his head to the side, exposing his chin.

Cassidy's voice came from right behind her. "Tristan is back in control. No dragon would ever expose the vulnerable, soft skin of his chin unless the human was calling the shots." The woman moved to Mel's side. "Calm him a little further and convince him to let my people near enough to heal him."

Mel was on the verge of tears, but managed to push them back and nod. Her job wasn't quite finished just yet.

She took a few more steps toward the dragon and said, "Tristan, let me touch your beautiful, smooth scales again. Blink if you feel I can do that without you hurting me."

The dragon slowly blinked and Mel's heart warmed. She fought the tears that threatened to fall and walked at a steady pace until she was less than two feet from the dragon. She raised her hand and slowly reached out until she could lay it on his snout. At the contact, the dragon gave a little hum.

She couldn't hold back her emotions any more. She whispered, "Oh, Tristan," before taking the last steps between them and then hugging his snout as she caressed the scales of his head and jaw. He might live.

She couldn't prevent her voice from cracking as she said, "Please let the healers help you. I don't want to live without you, you stubborn dragonman."

The dragon chuffed and Mel decided that was a yes.

Only through sheer will did she convince herself to let go of the dragon's snout. She quickly wiped her eyes before she turned and shouted, "He's okay. Come help him."

The healers didn't waste any time and rushed forth. Cassidy, their leader, told Melanie, "Stay to the right side of his head while we fix him. Your touch and voice will help ground him and, most importantly, keep the human-half in charge."

Mel nodded and moved out of the way, but she never severed contact with her dragon.

She looked into the huge dragon's eye in front of her and whispered, "I know you're all big and strong, but that wound has to hurt like hell and I want to help you forget about the pain. I'm not sure what to do, though, so I need your help. I'll try scratching and caressing certain areas, and blink twice if it's good or three times if it's not. Now, blink once if you understand."

The dragon blinked and Melanie smiled. "Good. I've always wanted to feel up a dragon." She winked. "Now, where to start..."

~~~

Thanks to Melanie, Tristan had managed to battle back into control of his dragon-half.

His human was cleverer than he'd realized. Her threat of walking away to find another male had been enough to drive his dragon crazy and to turn to Tristan for help, asking what they needed to do to keep her.

And now she wanted to touch, scratch, and caress his dragon hide. She really was a different type of human.

While waiting to see what Melanie would touch first— he hoped behind his ears, because it itched like hell— someone poured something into his wound and a blinding pain rushed through his body. What the fuck? Were they trying to kill him?

He gritted his teeth and just barely resisted roaring into his female's ear. His dragon pushed and growled to come out again. His beast said, *We need to knock the dragon-shifters away again. The pain is proof they are trying to kill us. They will use our weakness against us.*

Tristan growled inside his head. *Our female is right next to us. If we roar or thrash about, we will hurt her, maybe even kill her. Is that what you want?*

No. I never want to hurt her. She is our mate.

Then shut it and leave me alone for awhile.

His inner beast grudgingly retreated to the back of Tristan's mind.

As the pain dulled slightly, he could feel Melanie stroking his snout. His human said, "It was just some antiseptic. Stop acting like a big baby."

He tried his best to frown, but dragons didn't do facial expressions all that well.

Still, Melanie laughed and the sound helped to ease both the dragon and the man. She gave him a pat and said, "Men. No matter if they're human or dragon-shifter, they're all the same. If you're this bad when you're hurt, I hate to see what you're like when you catch a cold."

Tristan growled and decided right then and there he was going to live because he wanted to feel what it was like to have Melanie take care of him.

Something must've shown in his eyes because Melanie tapped his snout a few times and said, "Don't get any ideas. You have to be can't-get-out-of-bed sick before I start giving you any special treatment. Faking a headache isn't going to make me wait on you hand and foot."

He grunted in disappointment, not that he hadn't expected anything less.

Melanie waved a hand. "But now that you're acting yourself again, let's go back to the part of me getting to touch you." She ran a finger from his snout up to his eye ridge and scratched. "How about here?"

While it wasn't bad, he wanted her hands to keep going so he blinked three times. She frowned. "Okay, let's try something else. I know you're not a dog or cat, but how about here?"

She scratched behind his ear. He leaned into her touch and hummed in contentment. A dragon-shifter could learn to get use to this.

His inner dragon poked his head out again and said, *Yes, she is our mate. You must keep her. We love her.*

Tristan stopped humming and tried to process what his inner beast was saying. Yes, his dragon had been half in love with the human since the first day, but did the human part of him feel the same?

He didn't get the chance to think on it because Melanie stopped scratching as the clan's head doctor, a female dragon-shifter named Dr. Sid, came to stand in his line of sight. She said, "We've stopped the bleeding, Tristan, but I'll have to put you under to fix all of the damage. Nod if you will allow us to do this. The sooner I can cut you open and repair the rest of the damage, the better."

Tristan didn't like being unconscious in the hands of anyone, except maybe his human.

Then Melanie leaned against his snout and whispered into his ear, "I'll watch over you, Tristan, and make sure they don't try to sneak out any organs, or whatever strange dragon things are inside of you that I have no idea about."

He snorted. Like he had secret treasures stashed inside of him. His human could be silly.

But if Melanie watched over him, he would trust her not to let them harm him. She could stand up to just about any dragon-shifter if she put her mind to it.

For reasons he didn't want to think about right now, that made everything suddenly seem all right. He nodded to Sid and she turned her back to start ordering her team to get things ready for surgery.

In the meantime, he simply leaned against his human and into her caresses, wanting to memorize her touch. While his chances at living were better than before, he could still die. But the more Melanie accepted and maybe even cared for him, the more fuel it gave both him and his dragon to live.

CHAPTER TWENTY

Melanie paced in front of the large tent that had been constructed over Tristan's dragon-form for surgery. Cassidy—or, as most people seemed to call her, Sid—had finally kicked her out once she'd started cutting into the dragon. Not that Mel could blame her. Her little dragon baby had decided that the sight of blood and knives was not okay, and had thrown her a crippling wave of nausea.

Now that she was back outside in the fresh air, however, her stomach had settled, allowing her mind to whirl through all the possible outcomes. She dismissed half of them because she refused to believe Tristan would die.

At least most of the crowd had been sent home so she could fret in peace. She wasn't sure if everyone had left because the danger had mostly passed or because the tent blocked them from trying to take a peek. At any rate, she was glad they had left or she would've had to think of a way to get rid of them. Human or not, her dragonman was not to be eyed as some freak show accident to provide entertainment.

She had reached one edge of the landing area and was about to head back toward the tent when she heard a familiar deep voice. The words were a little faint and distant, but she could just make out, "We're nearly there. And see? Just like I told you. Everyone is gone."

Bram had finally decided to show up.

When he came into view, she marched toward him, about to demand what had taken him so damn long when she noticed Arabella beside him.

Mel blinked and stopped in her tracks. Arabella MacLeod was outside, and in the main living area no less.

Before she could get her mouth working again, Bram approached her and said, "You really should close your jaw or a bug might fly in."

Not realizing she'd had her mouth hanging open, Mel promptly shut it. Bram's words had kicked aside her shock and she frowned up at him. "What took you so long? I had a hell of a time of first getting to Tristan and then convincing the healers to let me calm him down. Your words could've made everything happen that much faster."

Rather than looking angry, Bram looked amused. "Your backbone never ceases to amaze me, lass."

She waved a hand in dismissal. As if she wouldn't do whatever it took to save Tristan's life. "Whatever. Tell me what happened."

Bram shrugged. "The mobile service signal at Ara's house is less than reliable, so I didn't hear about Tristan until you had already arrived and allowed the healers to work on him. Since you had things in hand, I decided to focus my energies on getting Ara here to see her brother."

Mel glanced over to Tristan's sister and noticed the woman was no longer in the strange trance-like state she'd been in earlier. If anything, the woman was frowning. Mel decided to go easy at first rather than incite the dragonwoman's temper. She could use Arabella's help against Sid and her healers if the doctor tried to keep information from her. "It's nice to see you again, Arabella. Tristan will be pleased."

She waited to see if Ara would simply ignore her or not. Thankfully, Bram also kept quiet.

After glancing to the tent and back, Tristan's sister said, "Why aren't you in there with him? They could be doing anything to my brother right now."

Mel resisted a smile at the dragonwoman's censure. "I was, but once the knives came out, little Tristan junior or junioress decided he or she wanted to leave. I figured vomiting on him wasn't the most sanitary of ways to show support."

Bram chuckled. She didn't dare hope for Ara to do the same, but the woman's frown eased a bit. At least that was something.

Ara said, "Who is operating on him?"

"Cassidy."

Ara nodded. "Good. Sid has the best reputation in the clan."

Mel didn't want to push her luck, but her curiosity pushed her to ask, "How do you know that?"

At first, Arabella said nothing. Since Mel knew how difficult this was for her, being out in the open and not fifteen feet away from a dragon no less, she didn't mind the woman's pauses. Hopefully, with time, they would lessen.

Finally Arabella said, "Word of mouth travels in cyberspace just as much as in real life." She scrutinized Mel from head to toe. "You're not taking the best care of yourself, let alone my future niece or nephew.

Convinced Arabella was no longer trapped in her memories like before, Mel wasn't going to tiptoe around Tristan's sister. That wasn't her style. "And when did I have the chance to do so?

I figured making sure my baby's father stayed alive was more important than finding something to eat."

To her surprise, Arabella nodded in approval. "I like your answer."

She stared. Maybe, just maybe, she and Ara would truly be friends one day.

Bram laid a hand on her elbow and started walking. He guided them toward some rocks lining the landing area and motioned for Mel to sit. "Ara's right, though. You should sit and I'll fetch something for you to eat and drink." He looked to Arabella. "Can you handle keeping Melanie company?"

Bram's tone had been strong, as if his question had been more an expectation than a request. Even Mel felt compelled to answer in the positive. She was beginning to understand this whole dominance thing.

Arabella dipped her head in the affirmative and Bram said, "Good. Call me if anything happens. Since I'm in the main area, I shouldn't have any more service interruptions."

With that, he was gone. Mel looked to Ara and patted the rock next to her. "Come. Sit down. I've been pacing for too long and it really doesn't help Tristan any."

Ara didn't sit. Instead, she said, "Thank you for saving my brother's life."

Mel blinked. She hadn't seen that coming.

She shrugged, downplaying her actions. "I'm sure he would've done the same for me." She patted the rock again. "Now, sit down. You're super tall and looking up at you is giving me a crick in my neck. My little dragon baby might not care, but I do. Sit down, Arabella. I won't bite."

SACRIFICED TO THE DRAGON

The dragonwoman hesitated a few second before gingerly sitting next to Mel. It took everything Mel had not to wrap her arm around the woman's shoulders for support.

But for now, she was content that Arabella MacLeod would sit next to her.

The two of them sat in silence, staring at the tent and no doubt both hoping Tristan would pull through.

~~~

Tristan was trying to sleep, but his inner dragon kept repeating, "*Wake up*" over and over inside his head. Nothing, not even a growl or a threat of not shifting for a week, would make the beast stop.

Finally tired of it, he cracked open an eye and promptly shut it again. He moved his arm over his eyes. The light was too bloody bright.

He heard a breathy, "Tristan," before a soft, warm hand grabbed his other hand and squeezed. He could scent Melanie Hall.

Suddenly, he remembered everything she'd done for him back in the clearing.

Clearly, he was still alive, and now in human form, which meant he was no longer in danger of dying. Yet he had no bloody idea what had happened between then and now. Maybe Melanie could tell him.

He moved his arm and opened his eyes more slowly this time to adjust to the light. Then he looked up into the face of his beautiful human. The way the light played along her cheeks and highlighted the red glints in her hair took his breath away. "Melanie."

His voice sounded more like a choke than his usual calm, deep voice. But before he could ask for water, Melanie threw her upper body against his and hugged him tightly.

Pain seared through his shoulder, and despite the surge of joy at her touch and warmth, he couldn't help but say, "Ouch."

"Oh, sorry!" She released him and moved away. His dragon growled at that, but Melanie then moved to stroke his forehead and both the man and beast settled down. His female smiled and said, "I would tease you about being a big man baby when it comes to pain, but I'm beyond happy that you're awake. You've been out for nearly a week, Tristan, and everyone was starting to think you wouldn't wake up."

The pain in his injured shoulder subsided as she continued to stroke his skin. He leaned into the caress of her fingers on his forehead and said, "But you never gave up, did you?"

A tear rolled down her cheek and he wished he had the strength to reach up and wipe it away.

Melanie shook her head as she rubbed away her tears. "No, of course not. If you haven't learned by now how stubborn I can be, then you never will."

His smile ruined his words. "You bloody stubborn ox."

She laughed and leaned down to kiss his lips. She lingered and he found the strength to raise his hand and cup her cheek. "Melanie."

"Yes?"

As they stared into one another's eyes, Tristan wondered what would've happened to him if Melanie Hall hadn't entered his life.

It wasn't just the fact she was giving him the chance to be a father or that the wound he'd received from the dragon hunters might've killed him without her coaxing and calming his dragon enough to let the healers help him.

There was also finding out the truth about Arabella and making him realize his sister needed more help than he'd offered.

And, most of all, Melanie Hall had convinced him that not all humans were bad. Yes, bastards like the Carlisle hunters deserved his hatred and scorn, but the average person deserved a chance. Some, such as his human, were downright amazing.

Before he could stop himself from asking the question burning in his mind, he said, "Why did you put up with me, Melanie? I was a right bastard to you. And as much as I recoil at the thought of another male touching you, I am honest enough to admit that you deserve a better man than me."

She frowned down at him. "That is your opinion. Do you want to hear mine?"

Yes, his dragon screamed. *Let her talk. Don't try to push her away. We love her.*

Rather than think on his dragon's use of "love" again, he nodded. Melanie sat on the edge of his bed and said, "You're partially right. You were a bastard." He opened his mouth to speak, but she beat him to it. "No, it's my turn to talk."

He shut his mouth and fought a smile at her bossy tone. The short, fragile human wasn't afraid to order him around, and both halves of him liked that. A lot.

Seeing that he was keeping quiet, Melanie sat up and continued, "But you were a bastard out of pain. Once I saw you interacting with the children, I knew there was a good man inside of you, buried beneath your animosity and anger. And since we were already tied together because of the baby, I decided it was worth fighting to see if I could help you. Your child will be half human, and I couldn't—and still can't—stomach the thought of you hating that part of him or her."

This time he wasn't about to allow her to think that of him. He said, "I could never hate our child because it will always be half you."

Her hand found his and squeezed. "Oh, Tristan."

He really should say more, but fancy, pretty words were not his forte.

His dragon-half, however, was pushing him to say more. *Tell her how we feel. Then we should claim her and never let her go.*

Tristan agreed with his beast. He didn't want Melanie to leave. Even if, for some reason, she didn't survive childbirth, he didn't think he could ever care as much for someone again as he did for Melanie Hall. Her stubbornness, determination, and love had won him over. Completely.

But just as he wrestled the nerve to say something, there was a knock on the door. Melanie quickly rubbed her eyes and said, "Come in."

Tristan had expected a doctor or maybe Bram. But it was neither.

His sister Arabella was standing in the doorway.

~~~

Over the past week, Melanie had won over Arabella bit by bit, but right now, she wished the dragonwoman would be anywhere but here.

Mel knew it was selfish, but Tristan was finally awake and she wanted to spend time with her dragon-shifter. Especially since the last of his inner walls constructed to keep her out were crumbling. His comment about never hating their baby because it was half hers had proven it.

But Arabella was Tristan's sister and she had spent a good deal of the last week relieving Melanie of bedside duty and making sure Melanie had food to eat. While Ara still acted self-conscious whenever a dragon-shifter stared at her scars, at least she wasn't cooped up in her house, locked away from the world.

And she had to be nearly as relieved as Melanie that Tristan was doing better. She smiled at the dragonwoman and said, "Did you hear? He's awake?"

She frowned. "Why didn't you call me?"

Mel still had a grip on Tristan's hand and squeezed it. "Don't look at me like that. It was only a few minutes ago and I think I earned a few minutes alone with my dragonman."

Tristan tugged at her hand and said, "Your dragonman is awake and can talk for himself. Can we stop pretending that I'm not here?"

She couldn't help but smile and motioned for Ara to join them before Melanie turned back toward Tristan. "There, now you're the focus of our attention again. Does that soothe your male ego?"

He frowned and Mel barely resisted laughing. He said, "I'm not awake five minutes and you're teasing me again. What happened to taking care of me? I think this qualifies as being unwell enough to merit it."

"If you think I'm going to coddle you and wait on you hand and foot, then you'll be waiting a long time."

Tristan smiled and Mel's heart skipped a beat. The man was beyond handsome when he smiled.

Before he could say a word, Arabella sat down on the other side of Tristan and said, "So I'm guessing that you're going to keep the human."

Melanie tried not to hold her breath as she waited for his answer. Every cell in her body screamed that Tristan cared for her and never would toss her aside, but he'd never said anything out loud and she desperately wanted to hear it. She wasn't a needy person by nature, but she'd like to know what her future held.

Well, at least for the next seven or eight months. She could still die in childbirth.

But she pushed that thought aside. Right now was a happy time. Tristan was awake and teasing her. Arabella didn't hate her and could stand being in her company. Things were good compared to when she'd first arrived here a few weeks ago. She could worry about dying later.

Tristan glanced at her before looking at his sister. "I'm not sure anyone could 'keep' her. You've seen what she's like. A right menace she is."

Mel's heart plummeted, but then Tristan looked at her with mischief in his eyes and hope surged again. He said, "But I plan on spending the time we have until our baby is born convincing Melanie to stay with me. Both the man and the dragon want to keep her."

She wanted to scream, "Yes!", but decided that would be a little too easy for her dragonman. After all, he'd admitted to being a bastard. She could tease him until he was well enough that she might reward him for not dying with more than words.

She tapped her chin in an overly dramatic fashion and said, "Hmm, well, you're going to have to work hard at convincing me to stay. You've been a bit mean since meeting me." She removed her finger from her chin and leaned down to whisper in his ear,

"But I hope that you spend a good chunk of your time convincing me to stay by being naked in my bed."

Arabella moved from the bed. "Okay, I really didn't need to hear that."

Oops. Mel had forgotten about the super-sensitive hearing of dragon-shifters.

She was about to apologize when there was a knock followed by the door opening to reveal Dr. Sid. "Someone reported hearing a male voice coming from this room despite the lack of male visitors, so I came to check and see if it was Tristan's." Her eyes darted to the male dragon-shifter. Then she looked from Melanie to Arabella and back. "And since he's awake, I need to do a thorough examination and ask some questions. I know he just woke up and you're happy about it, but I need you to leave me alone with him for fifteen minutes."

Before she could reply, Tristan spoke up, "Melanie needs to go rest and eat something anyway." She looked at his face and his eyes flashed to dragon slits. "My inner dragon doesn't like the circles under your eyes or the fact I can tell you've lost some weight this week. Go. Eat, rest, and get well for me."

"But you just woke up."

He squeezed her hand and looked to Dr. Sid. "The danger has passed, right, Sid?"

Mel looked over at the doctor and she nodded. "While a complete examination will tell me more, I'm fairly certain you should pull through just fine. We were concerned that you'd never wake up from your coma, but that worry is gone."

Tristan looked back to her. "See? Now that I'm getting better, I need you to take care of not only yourself, but our baby too."

Melanie was teetering. Now that she wasn't constantly worrying about Tristan, her exhaustion and hunger were starting to set in.

Still, she looked to the doctor and said, "Will the exam be able to tell you when he can come home?" The doctor nodded and she looked back to Tristan. "Okay, then you win this time. But after a nap and some food, I'll be back."

Tristan said, "Good. Wake me up if I'm asleep." She opened her mouth to protest but he shook his head. "No, Melanie. There are things we need to talk about and they can't wait."

She sighed. "Great. Now I'm sure that I'll sleep just fine with that sentence hanging over my head."

He snorted. "I'm not going to toss you aside or push you away again, if that's what you're worried about." He moved his hand to her thigh and squeezed. "Get some sleep. Then we'll talk about our baby and the future."

She moved her hand over his and squeezed. "Okay, okay. If sleeping will ensure that you'll talk openly later, then I can live with that deal." She leaned down and kissed him gently on the lips. She stayed a hairbreadth away and said, "Until later, dragonman."

The look in his eyes turned tender and sent a rush straight to her heart. She could still barely believe Tristan was finally hers.

She reluctantly moved from the bed and went out the door to allow Arabella to say goodbye to her brother. As she made her way to the exit of the building used as Stonefire's hospital, Melanie couldn't help but smile. Her dragon-shifter was awake, alive, and wanted to talk to her about their future.

Sacrificed to the Dragon

Maybe her stubbornness and ability to see the good in people were about to finally pay off. She hoped so because Melanie couldn't imagine living on Stonefire's lands to raise her baby without Tristan by her side.

Chapter Twenty-One

Tristan had tried sleeping once the doctor had left, but his dragon-half wasn't having it.

Our female is alone. No male to protect her. She doesn't know she's ours. Find her.

I've said it a million times. Soon. She's sleeping and we are still recovering. The dragon huffed and went back to pacing inside his head. No doubt so that Tristan would try to relax enough to fall asleep, only for his inner dragon to start demanding action all over again.

There were few times in his life he truly wished to silence his dragon, but this was one of them.

Did his dragon not realize how hard it was for Tristan to lie here, alone, without Melanie's scent or heat next to him? He wasn't well enough to fuck anything, but he wanted to hold his human close, and not just because he owed her his life. No, he missed her.

There was a gentle knock on the door before it eased open. Melanie peeked her head inside, but once she saw he was awake, she came in and closed the door behind her. She frowned and said, "Aren't you supposed to be sleeping?"

While he was happy to see his human's face again, he decided not to hide his grumpiness. "I tried to sleep, but my bloody dragon is all but roaring inside my head for me to find you."

"Oh."

"Yes, 'oh'. Come here, Melanie, and lie next to me."

She took a few steps closer, but remained out of the range of his hands and arms. "Not until you tell me what happened the day of Miles' rescue."

Right. The rescue. "That could take some time, love, and you look about ready to fall over."

She started to move toward him but caught herself. "How do I know this isn't a trick to get me into your bed and then you avoid answering any of my questions?"

This woman had risked her life to save his. Tristan was done with being anything less than honest with her. "My male ego may not like what happened, but you've earned an explanation. If not for you, Melanie Hall, I would not be alive. I will answer your questions. I swear it on our baby's life."

Melanie blinked, but then smiled. "I'm still trying to get used to this nicer version of you. It's a bit of a shock, really."

He growled. "I'm sure some of it will wear off when I'm not recovering from a near life-ending injury. Now, get into my bloody bed or I'll find a way to cart you over here myself."

She laughed. "I'd like to see that."

He tossed back his blanket and moved to sit up. Melanie put up her hands. "Okay, okay. I'll come over. Just don't try to get up or you might rip open your cut again."

She moved to his bed, sat down, and swung up her legs. The instant her head touched the pillow he threw his arm over her and squeezed. He whispered, "I've missed your soft body next to mine."

Her tone held warning. "Tristan, you're not well enough for sex. You know that."

He moved his head to lay it on her shoulder. He kissed the exposed skin over her collarbone. "Believe me, if I were, you'd already be naked and under me by now."

Her breath hitched and his inner beast hummed. *She likes the idea. Later, we'll take her over and over again. Then she'll never want to wander from us. She will stay forever.*

Quiet, he muttered at his dragon-half. *I can't think with you banging on around inside my head.*

The beast gave a huff and fell quiet, recognizing that it was the human-half of them who would have to convince their female to stay.

Melanie's soft, lyrical voice echoed beneath his ear. "Okay, so I know what the whole clan knows and that you had to help Kai and Zain rescue the teenager, who is bruised but alive and should be okay in time with the support of his family. But everyone was surprised you went into the Carlisle compound. Why? Everyone just dismisses a rescue as a Protector's job, not a teacher's. If that's true, why did they ask for your help in the first place?"

Apparently, his clan had kept more closed-lipped around Melanie than he liked. His dragon snarled at the lack of trust in their human, and Tristan nuzzled her exposed skin to calm both man and beast, loving the soft warmth of her skin. "The Protectors are similar to a human private security company. They're the best of the best and each of them has trained with the human military for a time. Usually, they are the ones to rescue or help get a dragon-shifter out of trouble. But the two young males who reported Miles' capture forgot to mention it was the Carlisle dragon hunters. Once we found that out, we had to change our plans and act fast."

"Why?"

He resisted tightening his grip around his human and instead leaned into her warm curves to keep his anger concerning the dragon hunters in check. The contact worked. "The Carlisle branch of dragon hunters will torture, abuse, and sometimes even rape a dragon-shifter before draining it of blood. The problem is, young dragon-shifter blood won't cure anything. They would either keep the young male until he was an adult, subjecting him to years of abuse, or kill him and sell his scales, teeth, and talons to the highest bidder."

"People still buy those things?"

Only because of Melanie's presence next to him did he keep his anger from his voice when he answered, "Yes."

She shuddered and he squeezed her in reassurance. Mel said, "Why didn't you wait for back-up? That seems like the most logical thing to do."

Yes, his human was clever. "Because if the Carlisle hunters had moved Miles to one of their secret locations, we might never have found him. There wasn't time to call for back-up, so despite my lack of training, Kai and Zain asked for my help and I couldn't say no when one of our young's lives was at stake."

"Of course you couldn't." Melanie laid her head on top of his. "So how did you get your injury?"

He grimaced and moved a hand to cover Melanie's lower abdomen. As much as he didn't want to admit his mistake, the mother of his child deserved to hear the truth. He said, "I was doing a sweep of their compound from the air while Kai and Zain did it on foot in their human forms. Normally, there's a certain height you can fly and avoid getting attacked by the hunters. But I didn't count on the Carlisle group having a newly developed weapon that could take a dragon out of the sky. It wasn't a missile, but more like a long-range laser that can slice through dragon scales. I wasn't quick enough to dodge it."

The memory of him being hit followed by the burning pain that had nearly taken him out of the sky rushed back and he tried not to wince. The new weapon was going to cause the dragon-shifters a lot of trouble in the future unless they could find a way to protect against it.

Melanie snuggled into his side and he leaned in to her touch. The reminder of his warm female banished the painful memory.

Since his human was being a little too quiet, he asked, "Are you okay? Is the baby making you nauseous again?"

"No. I'm just trying to contain my anger. How could the British government allow those poachers to still exist? Between the torture, rape, and now anti-dragon lasers, you think they would take care of it."

Her concern for his people warmed his heart.

He stroked her cheek. "If you're going to live with Stonefire, then you should know that until public opinion changes, the government will barely give a fuck about you and they care even less about the dragon-shifters. That includes our child."

~~~

Melanie was doing a pretty good job at keeping her temper in check. She'd known that the dragon hunters were bad, but Tristan was starting to give her a more complete picture of the day-to-day threat they posed to the dragon-shifters. What kind of person could torture and abuse a defenseless teenager?

Not only that, but hearing that the British government wouldn't help protect her baby because it was half dragon-shifter was the last straw. She needed to do something to change the status quo, and she might just have a way to do it.

She half-sat up and looked down at Tristan. "If Bram gives me a chance, I think I can change public opinion."

He frowned. "How do you plan to do that?"

Well, here goes. "I was being sincere when I mentioned to the children about wanting to write a book about the dragon-shifters. Now more than ever I think humans need something to help them move dragon-shifters from the 'abstract' to the 'very real'."

He stroked her hip as he said, "I don't doubt for a second that you could write a bloody fantastic book that would help us. After all, you managed to convince both me and my sister that not all humans are bad. But are you aware of the risks? The anti-dragon factions are quite brutal and will make you their number one target. Once that happens, it'll be near impossible for you to go off our land for quite some time."

The thought of never visiting Manchester's city center or the wilds of Scotland again made her heart ache, but she pushed it aside. The only thing she'd truly miss was her family, but maybe with time, Bram would allow them to visit, especially if they were targeted because of her efforts to help the clan.

She ran her hand up and down her dragonman's chest, needing the combination of his familiar hardness and heat to ease some of her worry. She finally replied, "If that's what it takes to ensure better treatment for my child, then so be it."

He squeezed her hip. "You are bloody amazing, Melanie Hall."

She smiled and blushed. She wasn't used to such praise from Tristan. "Does that mean you'll help me pitch the idea to Bram?"

"Pitch it? Hell, I'll tie him down if I have to. It's a brilliant idea and definitely merits a chance."

She full on grinned. "I'd like to see you try. Bram's quite dominant, you know."

He cupped her cheek and strummed his warm, rough finger against her skin. "For you, my little human, I'd chance it."

Tears prickled her eyes. Melanie had always been the champion of others. From the kids picked on at school, to her brother, to even Caitriona Belmont here on Stonefire's lands. Yet she'd never really had anyone want to champion and stand by her. The fact that her broody, alpha dragonman was willing to risk his clan leader's ire meant the world to her. For the first time in her life, she was beginning to think she might have someone to stand at her side and help her fight her battles. Someone to both encourage her and give her the truth when she needed to hear it. Someone to laugh or cry with when it came to her failures or successes.

And that person was the stubborn dragon-shifter lying next to her.

He had mentioned wanting to "keep" her, but in reality, she wanted to keep him.

Without thinking, she blurted out, "I love you, Tristan MacLeod."

His finger stilled on his cheek and she wondered if she had made a mistake. But Tristan rose up to kiss her and say, "Good. Then you're staying."

It wasn't exactly the romantic words you'd find in a movie, but considering her dragon-shifter, she didn't really expect it.

However, she'd be lying to herself if she didn't admit to feeling a little vulnerable and exposed by her admission and his lack of response.

But she had faith that maybe one day he'd come to love her too.

For now, she at least knew she would be able to stay with him and get to experience this nicer, teasing version of Tristan. Considering the uncertainty of her future, she would relish whatever she could take from life. She would make the next seven or eight months count.

Rather than think of dying, she just wanted to lie in the warmth and safety of her dragonman's arms.

Mel lay down, careful not to touch the opposite shoulder with his injury, and nuzzled into his chest. "Yes, I'm staying and we can talk about that more later. Right now, I'm exhausted and would love nothing more than for you to hold me close and sleep with me."

His voice rumbled under her ear. "That I can do."

He wrapped his arms around her and Mel let out a sigh. This was where she belonged, with Tristan MacLeod and his clan. She looked forward to him being hale and hearty so that he could give her some great "let's celebrate life" sex.

But as she breathed in the spicy male scent that was Tristan, she felt her eyelids growing heavy. There was a hell of a lot to think about and plan for, but without realizing it, she fell into a deep sleep next to the man she loved.

CHAPTER TWENTY-TWO

Melanie tried to sit down on the couch in the living room, but after about thirty seconds, she stood up and started pacing again. Tristan should be home from the hospital any time now, and she was a little nervous.

She wasn't worried about him acting differently now that he was healthy. Nor was she concerned about them trying to feel each other out as they tried to establish a daily, somewhat normal life. She'd spent most of the last week and a half in his company, and she was more in love with him than ever. Sure, he could still be alpha and broody, and he never gave up an argument without a fight, but that was just part of who he was. Besides, life would be pretty boring if he suddenly started "yes, dear"-ing everything she suggested.

But in between her visits to Tristan, Samira, Cait and even Arabella, she'd been working on a surprise for her dragonman. Bram had even helped her without hesitation to gather what she needed to pull it off.

Now all she had to do was wait for Tristan to get his ass home.

Her stomach flipped and she took a second to breathe in and out. She was not going to get sick. Not right now, not today. *Behave, dragon baby. Daddy's coming home. Let's make it a sick-free day. Yes?*

She didn't expect the tiny bean inside her uterus to listen to her, but it made her feel better all the same.

A few crackers and some water later, and she went back to pacing.

When the front door finally opened, she moved to stand a few feet from it. Tristan's tall, dark-haired self appeared in the doorway and she smiled up at him. "Hi."

Without a word, he moved inside the cottage, shut the door, and pulled her up against him. "As much as I love hearing your strange American-slash-slightly-British accent, I want more than that as a greeting."

She tilted her head and raised an eyebrow. "Oh? What in the world could you possibly want?"

He growled. "This."

And he kissed her.

She opened and welcomed him into her mouth. As she twirled and stroked against his hot, warm tongue, she leaned even more against him. But when his hands snaked under her silky tank top and stroked her skin, she pulled away.

Tristan growled. "The doctor cleared me. Wild sex in the forest will have to wait, but I've spent all week thinking of the many different ways I want to fuck you. I'm tired of only having you in my fantasies." Then his expression relaxed and took on a hint of worry. "Unless the baby is giving you trouble? Do you need to sit down? A drink of water? Some tea?"

She smiled at his concern. "The baby is behaving. For now, at least."

"Then what's wrong?"

She cupped his cheek. "Nothing is wrong, but before we have hot, earth-shattering sex, I have a surprise for you."

His eyes flickered to slits and back. "A surprise?"

She laughed. "I knew that would get your dragon's attention. Samira told me how dragons love surprises."

He grunted and she found it endearing.

She patted against his chest and pushed. He let her walk free and she retrieved the large, blue box from the coffee table. She turned toward him and took a fortifying breath. This was it. There was no turning back after this, but she didn't care. This was what she wanted.

She took a step toward Tristan and said, "My very first night here, at the First Kiss ceremony, your dragon sensed I was your mate." He looked curious, but nodded. Of course he would choose now to not interrupt her and let her talk. She took a deep breath and continued, "In the rare cases when a dragon-shifter finds his mate, it is not guaranteed that the male or female will accept the claim. I could walk away if I so choose, and you would have to let me go."

He frowned. "Yes, but—"

She interrupted him, afraid she'd lose her nerve. "Let me finish, Tristan." He nodded and she said, "I know it's only been about a month since we first met, and we've both been through hell and back, but as much as your dragon is possessive as hell about me, I'm starting to feel pretty possessive myself when it comes to you."

The corner of his mouth ticked up. "Is that so?"

She resisted the urge to tease him. She needed to get the words out. "Yes. And I want to make my claim official."

A flicker of longing flashed in Tristan's eyes, giving her the courage to open the box and say, "I accept your mate claim, Tristan MacLeod. Will you accept mine?"

He moved in front of her. "Will I? You bloody woman, do you even have to ask?"

"Hey, be nice. You haven't even looked at the arm cuffs. I went through a lot of trouble to get them engraved."

~~~

When Melanie had opened the box to reveal a pair of traditional dragon-shifter mate bands, Tristan's dragon had roared inside his head at the same time as happiness had flooded his body.

He could hardly believe it. Melanie wanted to be his mate.

All he wanted to do was take the box from her hands and toss it aside so he could kiss her and hopefully fuck her, but the frown on her face was adorable. Combined with his inner beast's dying curiosity—dragons really did like surprises—he couldn't resist looking down at the open box to get a better look.

Inside were two silver arm cuffs. One was larger and meant for him, while the other was more feminine. On his larger cuff was engraved, "Melanie's" in the dragon-language. His name was similarly engraved on hers.

Tristan had never imagined he would wear a human female's name on his arm, but now he couldn't picture anything else. Melanie Hall was his, and soon would be forever.

He traced the designs on the bands. In addition to the names written in the dragon language, they were also engraved with the bold, thick lines similar to Stonefire's chosen tattoo markings. The clan's silversmith, Dylan, must've made them. How Melanie had convinced Dylan to engrave these so quickly, he'd never know. But then his mate was always a force to be reckoned with.

She'd gone to such lengths to honor his people's traditions, and it touched both the man and the beast. For a split second, he wondered if he deserved her, but then his dragon said, *Of course. She is ours and we are hers.*

Aware that he'd been quiet for a while, he decided to find out how his human had known how to propose a mating. He looked up. "How did you know what to do? Since we only wear mating bands to celebrations and special events, their existence isn't common knowledge."

She lifted her chin and he resisted a smile at her sass. "You'd better start thinking more of my intelligence and resourcefulness, Tristan MacLeod, or I may just take the arm cuffs back."

A possessive streak roared through him. He wanted, no needed, to put his name on her arm. "No, love. I won't allow it. You've offered the mate claim to me and I'm taking it." He removed the band meant for him and snaked it around his tattoo-free bicep. It was snug, but not uncomfortable, which was fine considering it was only for special occasions.

His dragon crooned at having their mate's name around his arm. *The other males will leave her alone now. She belongs to us.*

More like we belong to her, he said to his dragon and his beast didn't disagree with that.

He removed the cuff meant for her and motioned toward her arm. "Melanie Hall, will you do the honor of becoming my mate?"

Her irritation eased and she lowered the box. "Of course, Tristan. Despite your moments, I love you."

She'd said those words to him once before, when he'd first woken up from his injury, and he'd yearned every day to hear them again. When she hadn't said them, he'd wondered if she'd only said them to him because of his nearly dying.

SACRIFICED TO THE DRAGON

But now neither of them was dying, and she'd said it so matter-of-factly that he knew it in his heart to be true. He felt the same, but had been waiting for the right time to tell her. He wanted her to know his feelings and not think it was simply out of gratitude for her saving his life.

Now was the time, and he couldn't hold back his feeling any longer. He said, "Good, because I love you too and a dragon-shifter in love is a force to be reckoned with."

Her breath caught. "Say it again."

He took the box from her hands and tossed it on the ground. "I love you, woman." He took her arm and snaked on the band. Then he traced his name on her arm before looking her in the eye. "Should I tell you the reasons why?"

She nodded and his dragon hummed. *It's about time she knows how we feel. Tell her nicely. It will make her happy, and our mate should always be happy.*

Ignoring his smug dragon, Tristan traced her brow with a finger. "I admire your cleverness and wit." He moved his hand down and traced her breast through her thin shirt, loving the fact she wasn't wearing a bra. Her nipple hardened under his touch. "I love every curve and valley of your body." He then moved his hand to her back and traced up and down her spine. "And I will always cherish your backbone and stubbornness, no matter how many gray hairs it might give me."

She slapped him lightly on the chest and he captured her hand with his own. He squeezed her fingers and said, "I love everything about you, Melanie Hall, and I will do everything within my power to make you happy." She raised an eyebrow at that and he grinned. "Okay, almost everything. I'm a stubborn bastard at times and it'll show through. But I don't think you want it any other way."

She smiled and moved her free hand up behind his neck. "No, I love you just the way you are. Now shut up and kiss me."

Tristan growled. He didn't need any more prodding and he took Melanie's lips in a rough kiss.

~~~

Because of her pregnancy hormones, Tristan's words had nearly made her cry. Rather than suffer the embarrassment, she'd taken the easy out and told him to kiss her.

As his lips nibbled hers before sweeping inside of her mouth, she was glad for choosing the silky tank top and skirt. His heat easily seeped into her skin, and she instantly went wet.

Tristan growled and she broke the kiss to whisper, "Do you want to know a secret?"

"What? Hurry up as my dragon is thinking of nothing but ripping your clothes off and fucking you. Hard."

More wetness rushed between her legs and her pussy started to throb.

Tristan growled again. "I can scent you. You have five seconds to tell me your secret before I rip off your clothes."

She gave a wicked smile. "That's the thing—I'm not wearing any underwear."

His nostrils flared and his eyes flashed to slits and back. He moved a hand to the edge of her short skirt and fingered between her thighs. Melanie moaned as he thrust a finger into her pussy.

"Fuck, you aren't," he said.

He swirled his finger around and she cried out. "Tristan, please. I've been waiting all week for you to fuck me again. I've missed you."

"With pleasure, my little mate."

He kissed her again as he removed his fingers and lifted her, cradling her ass with his large, warm hands. She tried rubbing against him, but he dumped her on the edge of the back of the couch and shimmied her skirt up above her belly. He then pushed her legs wide and rubbed his hands up and down her inner thighs.

He kneeled before her, confusing her. "What?"

He rubbed his hands on her thighs and looked up, his eyes heated and full of desire. "I said I'd fuck you, but I didn't say with my cock."

Before she could reply, his tongue was thrusting in and out of her pussy and she threaded her fingers through his hair to keep her balance. Moving her hips in time to his tongue, she decided that she could live with more of this. Lots more.

Then his tongue was gone and she dug her nails into his scalp in displeasure. She felt his chuckle against her thigh and his breath dancing across her pussy lips as he said, "I think we're both impatient to have my cock inside you. So I'm going to speed things up. You deserve pleasure first."

"Tristan."

Then his talented tongue was flicking and swirling around her clit, and she kept a grip on his head for balance. For the past week, she'd dreamt of Tristan licking between her thighs, but both her dreams and her memories were nothing compared to the hot, slickness of his tongue against her sensitive nerves.

She moaned as the pressure built, impatient for her first orgasm as mate to a dragon-shifter. Then Tristan bit her clit and she screamed as pleasure shot through her body, but rather than let her ride it out, Tristan plunged two of his thick fingers in her pussy and she clenched and released around him.

As she came down from her high, she hoped this was only the beginning because Tristan's tongue wasn't nearly enough. She was hungry for more. Much more.

~~~

Tristan gave his mate's clit one last swirl before he leaned back and looked up at her. Her eyes were heavy and half-lidded, just the way he liked it. Then the light glinted off the silver mate band on her arm and his dick pulsed. He wanted to fuck his mate while she wore his name on her body.

But first, he wanted to play a little more while his human-half was still in control.

He still had his fingers inside her pussy. Melanie had stopped spasming around him, and he widened his fingers and Melanie drew in a breath. "Tristan."

His dragon growled. *Take her. Remind her we are her mate. Brand our scent in her pussy.*

Just a few more moments and then we can do it your way.

His inner beast seemed content with that answer and sat back to see what would happen next.

Tristan closed his fingers and opened them again. In response, Melanie clenched the back of the couch on either side of her. With a gruff voice, he said, "I'm just trying to make sure you're ready for my cock, love, because I'm going to own your pussy like no tomorrow."

Melanie bit her lower lip and then looked down at him. Her voice was husky when she replied, "I'm ready, Tristan. Take me hard, the way your dragon likes it."

His dragon stood at attention at her words. *She thinks of both of us. We love her. No more playing. Take her now.*

SACRIFICED TO THE DRAGON

Tristan removed his fingers and gave them a lick. He growled in approval. He'd never tire of how bloody fantastic his mate tasted.

But his dragon was pushing harder to take control and Tristan wanted them to work together so they could both enjoy their mate.

He stood up, unzipped his jeans, and his aching dick burst free. Melanie's eyes moved to his cock, and he felt a drop of precum seep out.

His dragon growled. *It's been too long. Hurry up and fuck her. Hard.*

Tristan kicked off his shoes and jeans and moved between Melanie's thighs. She barely had time to hold on to his biceps before he positioned his cock and thrust into her.

She cried out but he barely noticed as he reveled in the feel of her tight, wet pussy. His dragon half urged him to move, but Tristan wanted access to her beautiful breasts first. He reached up, ripped off her tank top, and rolled her hard, pink nipple in his fingers.

As he pinched harder and watched her moan, the sight made his cock harder. She was bloody perfect.

His dragon huffed. *Yes, she is beautiful and she is waiting for us to take her. Do it already.*

Rather than fight his beast, he said to Melanie, "Are you ready for me, my little mate?"

"Yes, Tristan. Always."

"Good."

He let go of her nipple and took hold of her hips before he moved. With each thrust, he moved faster, never taking his eyes off his mate's eyes. She dug her nails in his biceps and he pounded harder.

His dragon hummed. *Yes. Harder. She belongs to us.*

From the corner of his eye, he could see her delicious curves bouncing in time to his thrusts, and the sight made him proud. He would make sure she knew how much he approved of her body.

Melanie clung to his arms and arched her back. From her little sounds of pleasure, he could tell she was close. He took a firmer grip on her soft, wide hips and thrust as hard as he could without crushing her. His dragon crooned, content with how they were taking their female.

Tristan felt the pressure building at the base of his spine. In the last second before he came, he took his mate's lips in a rough kiss, swallowing her cries as his semen made her come.

As her pussy squeezed and released his dick, he moved closer until he had his arms around her. When she finally sighed as her orgasm ended, he broke their kiss, stared into her eyes, and said, "You're mine, forever."

She smiled. "I think you're confused, Tristan, as you're mine forever."

He smiled and hugged his mate close. Never in a million years would he have expected to find such a wonderful mate he loved with every bone in his body. He only hoped he could love her until they were both gray and wrinkled.

They'd find out if he could have that dream or not in seven or eight months' time.

At the thought of Melanie dying in childbirth, he hugged her tighter. She mumbled, "What's wrong?"

Tristan didn't want to break the spell of their momentary happiness, so he said, "I'm just trying to think of what else my little mate can take before she's exhausted."

SACRIFICED TO THE DRAGON

Melanie hugged him tight and whispered, "Give me everything you've got, dragonman. I can take it."

With that he growled, and his dark thoughts disappeared as he thought of what else he wished to do. Since he wasn't always good with words, he decided to show her just how much he loved her with action.

EPILOGUE

Seven Months Later

Tristan MacLeod had experienced his fair share of pain, but the way Melanie was currently gripping his hand was one of the most painful experiences of his life.

Not that he could say so. As his mate's latest contraction finished, her grip relaxed and she deflated against the pillows. "I can't keep doing this, Tristan. We've been optimistic about me surviving the birth, but I'm pretty sure our babies are trying to kill me."

He hated the defeated sound of her voice. *Help her*, his dragon said. As if he wouldn't tear up the nearest mountain with his claws if it meant he could ease his mate's pain.

He smoothed her sweat-covered brow and placed a gentle kiss on her lips. "Don't you dare give up on me or our children, Melanie Hall-MacLeod. There is no bloody way I'm raising twins on my own. You'd better survive or I'll find a way to bring you back myself just to give you an earful."

Her weak smile warmed his heart. "You stubborn man. How many times do I have to tell you that your will isn't strong enough to do half of what you say."

He traced her cheek with his forefinger. "Well, this time I feel lucky."

She half-laughed, but then drew in a breath. "I think another contraction is coming."

SACRIFICED TO THE DRAGON

From the foot of the hospital-style bed, Dr. Sid spoke, "Okay, Melanie, we're nearly there. This time I want you to push with everything you have. Another push or two should do it."

Melanie shook her head. "I've been pushing for so long, Sid, and I can't keep doing this. I'm too tired."

Help her, his dragon repeated. *If we can't help her find her strength, we will lose her. We can't lose her. She is our mate.*

As if he didn't know that.

Tristan kept his worry bottled up inside him, however, and did what Melanie needed—he prodded her. "Come on, my little human. Are you really going to allow two tiny dragon-shifters to best you? You're months away from finishing your book. If you give up, it's much more than me whining about taking care of twins." He turned Melanie's face toward his, forcing her to look him in the eye. "It's even more than I will miss you and mourn you for the rest of my life, love. If you ever want your children to grow up in a world where humans might not be afraid of them, you need to live."

For a second, she said nothing. Then Melanie drawled, "Lay it on thick, why don't you."

His dragon piped in. *Good. Our human hasn't lost her spark. She will live. She must live.*

He pushed his dragon to the back of his mind to focus on his mate. "Grip my hand as hard as you like, but push with everything you have."

His mate took a deep breath and then nodded first to him and then to the doctor. She was definitely tired. Energy-filled Melanie would've made a remark about him trying to push an orange out of his cock to see how that felt.

In about thirty seconds, Melanie's contraction hit and she started screaming again. It took everything Tristan had to keep his dragon from snarling and taking over.

Sid said, "Good, good. I see the head." The doctor looked up. "Do you need one contraction to rest or do you want to push harder and get the baby out?"

Melanie panted as the contraction ended. "A break. Please."

The exhaustion in her voice went straight to his heart.

She'd been in labor for about thirty hours. Tristan hoped it would be over soon. His mate needed to rest.

He wiped her brow with a cool cloth and whispered, "Nearly there, love. Do you think the boy or the girl will come first?"

She glared at him, and he was glad to see a shadow of her normal spirit. She spat out, "I don't fucking care which one. Just get it out of me."

He grinned and she narrowed her eyes further at him a second before her next contraction hit. She yelled and Tristan did his best to comfort her. When it finally ended, she whispered, "I'm pushing on the next one or I won't be able to do it."

He nodded. "You can do it, my brave little human."

She closed her eyes for about ninety seconds until the next contraction hit. Then she opened them as the doctor said, "Push!"

His mate gripped his hand as she screamed and after a few seconds, Sid smiled and looked up. "Your first child is a boy."

The nurse at Sid's side helped Sid before raising their baby so they could see his chubby little face.

Tristan had a son.

He was pink and tiny, and both the man and beast wanted nothing more than to hold him. But as the nurse nodded and took him away, he turned back to Melanie and kissed her. "Good job, my little mate. We have a son."

Melanie looked happy despite her exhaustion. "I'm glad."

Then another contraction hit and Sid said, "I know you're tempted, but don't push right now, Mel. I need to check the second baby's position."

Melanie gritted her teeth and clenched his hand. His dragon roared at the amount of pain she was in. Watching her suffer and not being able to do a damn thing about it tore apart both the man and the dragon.

Unlike with human children, dragon-shifter babies often died if the mother received any type of anesthetic, which ruled out both epidurals and C-sections. His human hadn't had a choice but to deliver naturally or risk losing both of their children.

And given her personality, she hadn't hesitated two seconds before agreeing to the natural birth despite the risk to her own health.

So far her blood pressure and toxin levels were within normal range, but that could change any moment.

No. She was his mate. She wouldn't die.

He continued to caress Melanie's cheek as the doctor prodded her protruding belly. When Sid cursed, Tristan's dragon stood at attention. "What is it?" he demanded.

"The second baby's breech. I had hoped she'd turn around after her brother came out, but apparently she's being stubborn. I need to try turning her since it's easier than delivering breech. Whatever you do, Melanie, do not push. Don't do it."

Melanie nodded and clenched her jaw. Tristan laid his forehead against hers and whispered, "Hold on, my strong, beautiful human. We're halfway there."

She let out a hiss. "You do this to me again and I will cut off your cock, Tristan MacLeod. Two children had better be enough."

He would rather cut off his dick than suffer through this again, wondering each second whether she would live or die.

But right now, he pushed aside his fears. His mate needed humor more than anything. "We're about to have two smaller copies of you. I don't think I could handle any more mini-Melanies running around."

She was about to scold him but he grinned and she gave a weak laugh. "An army of Melanies. That would definitely keep you on your toes."

"And knowing your stubbornness, you'd say screw the odds and have more girls."

Melanie smiled but then winced at whatever the doctor was doing to try to turn the baby. He kissed his beautiful mate. "To distract you, let's try to agree on a name for our son since we still haven't decided on one yet."

And much like they had done for the past three months, they argued about baby names.

~~~

An hour later, Melanie was pretty sure she was going to die.

She kept falling asleep for a few seconds and waking back up again. The contractions kept coming, but the doctor kept telling her to wait. Then the nurse's expression as she checked the monitor next to her kept getting worse with each passing minute.

If it weren't for Tristan, she might have given up half an hour ago. But as he continued to caress her brow, her cheek, and her jaw, his fingers gave her the strength she didn't think she had.

However, she was getting close to her limit. She wondered if Caitriona Belmont had felt the same way right before she'd died in childbirth four months ago.

No. She wouldn't think of her friend's death right now. Melanie wanted to live for Tristan, for their children, and most of all, for herself.

After riding out another contraction and seeing the growing worry on the nurse's face, she decided to fuck it. If she was going to die, she wanted to know the truth. Her voice was weak to her own ears when she asked, "The nurse looks worried. What's wrong?" She glanced to Dr. Sid. "And don't lie to me."

Sid replied, "Your blood pressure is rising and thanks to birthing one baby and not the other, the level of dragon-shifter toxins in your blood is getting higher than I'd like."

She vaguely remembered being told that when under stress or duress, dragon-shifter babies in utero could release a toxin that she would absorb. In dragon-shifters, it caused mild nausea. In humans, it could kill them.

No doubt her little girl was stressed because of the long labor and at losing her womb-mate. She'd been alone for nearly an hour now.

Tristan squeezed her hand and said to the doctor, "You haven't been able to turn the baby. Can't you deliver it breech?"

Sid looked grim. "Yes, it's looking like your daughter is being stubborn. I wonder where she gets that from."

Melanie managed enough energy to smile and said, "Her father" at the same time Tristan said, "Her mother."

She glanced at Tristan and took strength from the love shining in his eyes. She squeezed her mate's hand and said, "This is just the beginning. You know they're going to be little hellions, right?"

"As long as you're there to help me, I don't care how much trouble they are."

She so very much wanted to be there, but if she couldn't push out her daughter soon, she knew she may not make it.

Sid moved down between her legs again and said, "I'm going to help the baby along. What I'm about to do may be uncomfortable."

Before she could reply, she felt something in her vagina and Mel clenched her teeth. She could swear it was the doctor's hand.

Tristan murmured into her ear until the doctor said, "Okay, on this next contraction, we're going to work together. Don't push right away, but do it when I say push."

She nodded and gripped Tristan's hand even tighter. She breathed in and out, in and out. Then the contraction hit her and she screamed.

"Don't push yet!"

She hurt so badly and every instinct in her body told her to push. Tears flowed down her cheeks and she was vaguely aware of Tristan caressing her cheek.

"Push!"

And Melanie let out a yell as she pushed as hard as she could. When she finally felt the baby slip out of her body and let out a cry, she glanced to Tristan before the world went black.

~~~

Tristan heard their daughter's first cry and was about to kiss his mate when Melanie's hand went slack.

Both the man and beast yelled, "No. No, no, no."

He glanced to the monitor and saw a weak heart rate moments before it went flat.

234

He squeezed Melanie's hand. "Love, wake up." He looked to Dr. Sid. "Help her."

Sid and the nurses were already in action. Sid came to his side of the bed and pushed him away. "Leave the room, Tristan."

His inner dragon growled. "I won't leave her."

Sid gave him a commanding glare. "I don't have time for your alpha protective bullshit. Get out or let Melanie die. Take your choice."

His dragon was clawing to get free, but Tristan pushed him back knowing full well that if his beast took control, Melanie would die.

Through sheer force of will he released his mate's hand and moved out of the way. He let a nurse guide him out of the room, never taking his eyes off his mate until they were out in the hall.

He stopped and clenched his fists. He wanted to do something to help her, but in this, he was useless. Especially as his dragon was threatening to come out and kill everyone in the delivery room. His beast snarled and said, *They killed our mate. We must avenge her.*

Shut it, he yelled at his dragon. *They are trying to save her.*

His dragon gave a grunt and went back to pacing.

The nurse touched his arm and he glanced over. "Do you want to see your children now?"

With his dragon pacing and growling inside his head, seeing his children would help to keep his human-half in control. Not only that, it would help distract his human-half as well. He had every confidence in Sid's abilities. Between the skill of the doctor and his mate's stubbornness, he was confident Melanie would come back to him.

She had to.

He nodded at the nurse and followed her down the hallway into the newborn room. Since dragon-shifter numbers were low, there weren't any other children in the room.

As he approached the two little carts that held them, he could scent his son and daughter and his dragon relaxed a fraction. *We must protect our young. We won't let anyone harm them.*

Tristan didn't argue and reached a hand out to caress the cheek of his son and then his daughter. And for the first time in memory, he felt tears prick his eyes. He whispered to his children, "Don't worry. Your mum will be a bit late, but she'll be here. She loves you and would never abandon you."

As the feel of his children's skin helped to calm him, he only hoped he wasn't lying.

~~~

Melanie heard a voice so faint she couldn't make out whether it was male or female, let alone what they were saying. There was so much noise. Beeping and yelling. Metal crashing and more yelling.

But she didn't hear the cries of her children.

Her children. Where were they?

Then she felt a jolt go through her body followed by a split-second burning, which caused her to gasp in a mouthful of air. She opened her eyes and saw four dragon-shifters standing around her.

As her muddled mind tried to figure out what was going on, one of the dragonwomen—the doctor, she remembered—said, "Melanie. Thank fuck. Can you hear me?"

It took a colossal amount of energy for her to whisper, "Sid?"

"Yes, it's me. You're going to be okay."

"Tristan?"

"He'll be back soon. You know how protective male dragon-shifters are, so I kicked him out. He's with your children."

Her children. She wanted her children. "Where are my babies?"

Sid said, "We'll bring them in shortly. I think you're out of the danger zone, but I want to monitor you for the next ten minutes just to make sure and also deliver the afterbirth. It's safe for you to fall asleep, so close your eyes and I'll wake you when Tristan comes back with your twins."

She whispered, "Tristan," before her eyes slid closed. After nearly a day and a half in labor, she couldn't help but fall asleep.

A short time later, she woke to someone shaking her. "Melanie, wake up. Tristan's here."

At the sound of her mate's name, Melanie forced her eyes open. Her brain was still bleary with exhaustion, but her power nap had helped with her concentration.

The doctor moved out of the way and she saw Tristan holding two little bundles.

The picture of her tall, muscled dragonman holding two tiny, ridiculously pastel bundles in green and yellow made her smile. "Hi," she whispered.

Tristan rushed to her side and maneuvered himself into the chair at her bedside. He leaned over and kissed her before he said, "Hi, yourself."

"You're being nice to me. It's weird."

He smiled. "Don't worry, it won't last long. Now, how would you like to meet your children, Melanie Hall-MacLeod?"

Tears filled her eyes and she nodded. He raised one bundle, the yellow one, and said, "This is our daughter," —he then raised the green bundle— "and this is our son."

She was too exhausted to attempt picking up either of her children. Instead, she said, "Can you place one in the crook of my arm, Tristan?"

"I can do better than that."

He rearranged her arm and placed their daughter. Then he gently laid their son on her chest and kept him steady by supporting him with his hand.

At the feel of the warmth of her two children, tears rolled down her cheeks. Happy seemed too tame a word to describe what she felt right now.

As she looked from her son to her daughter and then up to her mate, she decided she felt complete.

Tristan kissed her, lingering a few seconds before pulling away. "Sid told me we only have a few minutes before I need to let you rest. So I wanted to tell you our children's names first."

She frowned. "Tell me? Since when do you get to decide?"

He grinned. "I think you will like my names."

She doubted it, but she was too tired to argue. "Fine. What ridiculous names did you decide on? Gerard and Millicent?"

"No." He nodded toward their son. "This is Jack Ryan." He then nodded toward their daughter. "And this is Annabel Piper."

Melanie blinked. "But those are the names I wanted."

He smiled and caressed her forehead with his free hand. "You more than deserve the privilege of naming them, love. I think I can live with my children being named Jack and Annabel MacLeod."

Tears started falling again and Mel somehow managed to whisper, "Are you sure?"

"Of course. I already registered their names with the nurse, so it's a done deal."

"Oh, Tristan."

He leaned down and kissed her. Then he laid his forehead on hers. "All that matters to me is that my family is alive and healthy. Our children's names mean little as long as I have you."

Love spread throughout her body. "Tristan MacLeod, I love you."

He smiled. "And I love you too, my little mate."

As they smiled at each other, their daughter started to fuss so Tristan stood up. "I think the nurse is going to help you feed the baby. And then I'm kicking the nurse out so you can get some sleep."

"But you'll stay with me and the babies?"

"Always."

Melanie was really doing the waterworks today, but given the amount of hormones currently surging through her body, she decided she could cry as much as she wanted.

When the nurse came over, Tristan gingerly picked up their son Jack, moved out of the way, and traced the little man's cheek. The sight of Tristan MacLeod, alpha dragon-shifter extraordinaire, cooing a baby warmed her heart.

She hugged her daughter close and decided that she and Tristan had come a long way. What had originally started out as an exchange to save her brother's life had turned into her own happily ever after.

Not that times wouldn't be tough in the future, especially once she finished her book, but Melanie had her own family now and she would do whatever it took to protect them. She didn't doubt for a second that Tristan would do the same. Together, they might be able to make the world a better place for their children.

For now, she watched her mate and cuddled her daughter, content to live in the moment because she'd never been as happy as she was right at that moment.

Dear Reader:

Thanks for reading *Sacrificed to the Dragon*. I hope you enjoyed Melanie and Tristan's story. If you're craving more of this couple, then know they do have a follow-up novella later in the series (*Revealing the* Dragons). Also, if you liked their story, please leave a review. Thank you!

The next book is about Stonefire's leader, Bram Moore-Llewellyn, and is called *Seducing the Dragon*. Turn the page for the synopsis and an excerpt.

To stay up to date on my latest releases, don't forget to sign-up for my newsletter at www.jessiedonovan.com/newsletter.

With Gratitude,
Jessie Donovan

Seducing the Dragon
(Stonefire Dragons #2)

On her first visit to Clan Stonefire, Department of Dragon Affairs inspector Evie Marshall has an ulterior motive--she needs to seduce its clan leader. If she can't seduce him and become his mate, the dragon hunters will kill her. Of course, Evie doesn't know the first thing about seducing a man, let alone a dragon-shifter, but with her life on the line, she's going to have to become a fast learner or die trying.

Bram Moore-Llewellyn has a track record of scaring off DDA inspectors, but when the latest inspector shows up wearing tight clothes and a sexy smile, his inner dragon takes notice. While battling his attraction to the human, he soon finds himself with an impossible choice: he can either break the law to mate the female and risk a backlash from both the dragon hunters and the British government, or he can turn her away and let her die at the hands of the hunters.

Excerpt from *Seducing the Dragon*:

CHAPTER ONE

Evie Marshall pulled her car into the parking area next to Clan Stonefire's main gate and willed her stomach to settle. Sure, she was nervous, but it wasn't because of the dragon-shifters flying overhead or the glares she knew she'd face once she stepped onto their land. She'd worked the last seven years with the Department of Dragon Affairs down in London, and visiting a dragon clan's land wasn't anything new.

Yeah, right. Who was she kidding? Today was different from her other visits. She was here to seduce a dragon-shifter, and not just any dragon-shifter, but Stonefire's clan leader, Bram Moore-Llewellyn.

That was her goal, anyway. Whether she'd succeed or not was yet to be seen.

Her heart skipped a beat at the thought of failure. If she couldn't convince Bram to allow her to stay with the dragon-shifters then the dragon hunters would kidnap her, and maybe even kill her. Their warning last week had been clear: stop working for the Department of Dragon Affairs and join them or be hunted down as if she were a dragon herself.

Inhaling in and out repeatedly, she tried to pull herself together and push aside her fear. The British government had brushed off the threat and wouldn't help her, so she'd do whatever it took to seduce Bram and earn a place in his clan. Rumors said he was civil with humans, and if she could make him care about her, the alpha dragonman would protect her.

Focus, Evie. Right. Glancing at the clock on the console, she realized she needed to get a move on. From her past experiences down south with Clan Skyhunter, she was aware that while dragon-shifter clan leaders liked to keep her waiting, she had damn well better be on time or face a scolding.

After giving her hair one last smooth and plumping up her slightly too small breasts, Evie grabbed her duffel bag and exited the car. As she closed the distance between her car and the front entrance, it took everything she had not to stumble or twist her ankle on the uneven gravel. She'd worn heels maybe ten times in her life, and despite the hours of practice she'd done over the last week, she wobbled more than strutted with each step.

Shit. Things weren't off to the greatest of starts.

Careful to walk slowly and not fall on her arse, she headed toward the stone structure about twenty feet away, which served as the clan's security checkpoint. Since employees from the Department of Dragon Affairs, or DDA, weren't allowed to drive onto Stonefire's land, Evie went to the smaller entrance and called out, "Hello?"

Soon, a tall man with light blond hair and the ever-impressive thick, twining dragon-shifter tattoo on his muscled arm approached. She might've worked with the dragon-shifters for years, but her heart rate always kicked up when she saw one. They must have some kind of special gene which made them all gorgeous. This man was no different. The way his low-slung jeans clung to his fit body made her a little wet.

If she were lucky, Bram would be a little less attractive. The last thing she needed was to go instantly wet in his presence and start thinking with her lady parts instead of her brain.

The blond-haired dragonman's voice interrupted her thoughts. "Ms. Evie Marshall with the Department of Dragon Affairs?"

Careful to keep her face calm and collected, despite the butterflies banging around in her stomach, she nodded and handed over her identification papers. "Yes. I'm here to do my post-birth interview with Melanie Hall and to further investigate the death of Caitriona Belmont. My office should've made all of the arrangements for my three-day visit."

The dragon-shifter gave her an unreadable glance before he thumbed through her documents. No doubt, he could hear her heart banging in her chest, or even worse, smell the fact she found him attractive. While he was probably used to the latter, she hoped the former wouldn't raise any suspicions about her reasons for being here.

Only when he nodded and held out the papers for her to take back did she let out a mental sigh of relief. He must believe she was merely here for an inspection.

She retrieved her papers, and then he turned and motioned to another guard a few feet away. "Dacian over there is your assigned guard for the duration of your visit and he'll take you to see Bram."

At Bram, the clan leader's name, her heart gave a few extra hard thumps inside her chest. In less than half an hour, she would finally meet the man who would determine her future.

"Thank you," she said and smiled over at the dark-skinned man named Dacian.

And damn, the defined muscles peeking out from his shirt combined with the striking planes of his face only confirmed her theory of the secret dragon-shifter hotness gene. Her chances of Bram being less attractive so she could focus were looking slimmer by the minute.

Despite her best smile, his face was guarded as he motioned with his head for them to start walking. Without so much as a word, he turned around and headed down the worn dirt path.

Hmph. Stonefire's reputation about being friendlier with humans than Skyhunter wasn't looking good so far. She bloody well hoped Bram was nicer than Skyhunter's leader, Marcus, or she would most definitely have her work cut out for her.

Since Dacian was already several feet ahead of her, Evie tried her best to both walk quickly and sway her hips in what she hoped was a seductive manner. Her two-inch heels were less than ideal for a lengthy walk to the main living area, but first impressions were important. She would gladly risk sore feet if it meant Stonefire's leader would take notice of her.

Of course, her feet were the least of her problems. Evie had sacrificed a social life, hobbies, and even love to earn a place with the DDA, but those sacrifices now paled in comparison to the task that lay before her. In order to stay alive, she would have to give up not only her body, but also her freedom and her future.

~~~

Bram Moore-Llewellyn attempted to sign his name on the last bit of paperwork for the DDA inspection when he heard a "whoosh" followed by a little baby hand slapping against his desk. With a sigh, he tossed his pen aside and turned wee baby Murray around in his lap before raising him to eye level. "What did we say about knocking papers off the desk?"

Murray looked at him with wide eyes and drooled.

Bram chuckled. "Right, I know you're bored, but the inspector should be here any time now and she needs to see you're doing well."

The baby waved his hands around and started to squirm, clearly not caring about any DDA inspection. Bram lifted the boy above his head and said, "Just another half hour or so, lad, and I'll drop you off at my brother's house where you can play with my niece. You like Ava, remember?"

Murray made some incomprehensible baby noises and Bram took that as a yes. He lowered Murray down and cuddled him against his chest. His inner dragon pushed to the front of his mind and said, *We should keep this young. He is ours.*

He wanted to agree with his dragon, especially since Bram's chances of having children were less than one percent because of infertility issues, but it wasn't what was best for the lad. *He deserves someone with time to take care of him. We are too busy.*

His dragon huffed and Bram resisted a sigh. He'd been having this inner argument for months now. Taking care of a clan with nearly three hundred dragon-shifters was enough of a challenge, but it became infinitely harder to manage his people when his dragon became grumpy and uncooperative.

So much for Bram being bloody good at controlling his beast.

There was a knock on the door and Bram looked down at Murray. "All right, lad, I bet that's the inspector. Be on your best behavior, okay?"

While all the boy did was blink as he gnawed on his fist, Bram hoped the undertone of dominance in his voice would do the baby some good. Like most young, Murray had good days and bad.

Bram hoped today was one of the good ones or no doubt the inspector would make his life hell. Hate was too tame a word for what Bram felt about being beholden to the British government for his clan's survival.

He reached the door and opened it to find one of his guards, Dacian, filling his front stoop. Bram nodded to signal all was well, and Dacian stepped aside. His actions revealed a red-haired human female wearing a light blue blouse that hugged her small breasts, and her wide hips were encased in a black form-fitting skirt. Her dark blue eyes reminded him of the Irish Sea.

As she glanced between him and the baby, surprise flickered and Bram fought a smile. According to his contacts, this woman had been dealing with Marcus, Skyhunter's bastard leader, for years and would never expect a clan leader to answer a door with a baby in his arms.

However, the surprise in her eyes was gone in an instant, replaced with a smile and a look of heat that took both the man and the dragon by surprise. Even his cock twitched at the fiery look.

The redheaded female gave him a slow once over and he came back to his senses. Sure, she was pretty and plump with striking dark blue eyes, but he didn't need this right now. Between selecting a male from his clan to breed with the next human female sacrifice and doubling his clan's efforts against the recent spate of dragon hunter attacks, he didn't have time to bat off a female's attentions. When Bram wanted sex, he found it. He didn't need a mate.

His inner beast growled. *Liar.*

Sacrificed to the Dragon

Ignoring his dragon, Bram shuttered his face, hugged Murray closer to his chest, and motioned with his head. His voice was full of dominance when he said, "I have the necessary paperwork inside. Follow me."

He turned without another word. The sooner he finished this interview, the sooner the DDA inspector could leave and become some other male's problem.

Want to read the rest?
Seducing the Dragon is available in paperback

For exclusive content and updates, sign up for my newsletter at:

http://www.jessiedonovan.com

AUTHOR'S NOTE

I never expected people to enjoy my dragon-shifters this much, and I'm grateful every day for the support of my readers and fans! I have many more stories to tell in this world, and I hope you'll join me along for the ride.

However, I had a lot of help in getting this story out and I would like to thank a few people.

I am extremely grateful to Becky Johnson of Hot Tree Editing for responding to my, "Hey! I have a new idea! Can you book me in the next few weeks for this awesome story I'm going to write now?" with a "Sure, we'll make it work." Becky and her team have made me a better writer.

I also need to thank Clarissa Yeo of Yocla Designs for my gorgeous covers. I asked for a hot guy and a dragon on the cover, and she came back with the eye-catching red cover we all know. She is extremely talented, and I am lucky to have her as my cover artist.

Jayelle Anderson was my "beginnings" critique partner for this book. It was because of her questions that I was able to make my world-building more believable. She has an awesome web comic, Anaria, and you should check it out (Anaria.net).

Thanks everyone! If you don't completely hate me for killing off Caitriona Belmont (sorry, it had to be done! It'll make sense eventually…), then I hope you'll join me for Bram and Evie's story, *Seducing the Dragon*.

Happy reading!

ABOUT THE AUTHOR

Jessie Donovan wrote her first story at age five, and after discovering *The Dragonriders of Pern* series by Anne McCaffrey in junior high, she realized people actually wanted to read stories like those floating around inside her head. From there on out, she was determined to tap into her over-active imagination and write a book someday.

After living abroad for five years and earning degrees in Japanese, Anthropology, and Secondary Education, she buckled down and finally wrote her first full-length book. While that story will never see the light of day, it laid the world-building groundwork of what would become her debut paranormal romance, *Blaze of Secrets*. In late 2014 she officially became a *New York Times* and *USA Today* bestselling author.

Jessie loves to interact with readers, and when not reading a book or traipsing around some foreign country on a shoestring, can often be found on Facebook:

http://www.facebook.com/JessieDonovanAuthor

And don't forget to sign-up for her newsletter to receive sneak peeks and inside information. You can sign-up on her website:

http:///www.jessiedonovan.com

CPSIA information can be obtained at www.ICGtesting.com
Printed in the USA
LVOW12s2324140216

475103LV00003B/77/P